KU-325-164

144

THE 12-GUN CUTTER

Michael Fitton fell in love at first sight with the armed cutter *Snipe*. She was beautiful and seaworthy, with a happy crew and a competent if enigmatic captain. Originally they were due to sail from Naples to Gibraltar—an unexciting prospect, until a last-minute re-routeing sent them on a hazardous mission to enemy-held Minorca, complicated by the advent of the high-spirited Luisa O'Brien. Mr Fitton's stoic philosophy, as well as his seamanship, withstood a series of trials until, at last, he found himself leading *Snipe*'s crew in their desperate fight with a Spanish frigate.

THE 12-GUN CUTTER

THE 12-GUN CUTTER

by
Showell Styles

Magna Large Print Books
Long Preston, North Yorkshire,
England.

British Library Cataloguing in Publication Data.

Styles, Showell
    The 12-gun cutter.

    A catalogue record for this book is
    available from the British Library

    ISBN 0-7505-1146-X

First published in Great Britain by Robert Hale Ltd., 1996

Copyright © 1996 by Showell Styles

The right of Showell Styles to be identified as the author
of this work has been asserted by him in accordance with
the Copyright, Designs and Patents Act, 1988

Published in Large Print 1997 by arrangement with Robert
Hale Ltd.

All rights reserved. No part of this publication may be
reproduced, stored in a retrieval system, or transmitted in any
form or by any means, electronic, mechanical, photocopying,
recording or otherwise, without the prior permission of the
Copyright owner.

515168

MORAY DISTRICT COUNCIL
DEPARTMENT OF
LEISURE AND LIBRARIES
F

Magna Large Print is an imprint of
Library Magna Books Ltd.
Printed and bound in Great Britain by
T.J. International Ltd., Cornwall, PL28 8RW.

Contents

1 Lady Hamilton Disposes

1

Michael Fitton never met Lady Hamilton, though he was to hear a great deal about her in the years that followed the Battle of the Nile. Emma Hamilton never heard of Michael Fitton; it was in any case highly improbable that the wife of the British Envoy at the Court of Naples would have even hearsay acquaintance with an obscure master's mate. Yet it was through Lady Hamilton that the 12–gun cutter with Mr Fitton aboard was dispatched on her eventful mission and the destinies of more than one of her ship's company changed.

Early on a September morning Emma came out through the great doors of the Palazzo Sessa into the pillared portico and paused to survey the immense view of sea and sky. The Palazzo, Sir William Hamilton's residence, stood high above the port of Naples with its steep cobbled alleys and fetid stinks, and there was little to be seen of the quays far below her, but the vast blue plain of the sea stretched away to a clear horizon, and it was the white sails that dotted it here and there that attracted Emma Hamilton's gaze. Until lately she hadn't cared much for the sea. But now she was seeing herself as a woman destined to have much to do with the sea and sailors; one sailor in particular.

She stood with one uplifted hand resting against the fluted marble of the pillar, and the pose was singularly graceful, as she was well aware; there was no one to see her, but the habit of posing was second nature with Emma now.

She wore a simple dress of flowing white with a narrow sash of dark blue at the waist, and her bright auburn hair was bound with a blue fillet on which the words NELSON AND VICTORY were embroidered—she had made it herself. The heart-shaped face that had charmed so many men was a trifle fuller at cheek and neck than it had been when Romney had painted her as Circe, but it was still beautiful, and if there was more amplitude above and below the blue sash now than there had been then it was as yet no more than would have contented a Juno. Something of this was in her mind as she came lightly down the wide steps to the carriage-drive and paused there to adjust the sash, which was too tight, with a rueful little smile.

The Palazzo Sessa raised its impressive façade on a shelf of the Phlegrean hills, standing so close under the slope that at this early hour the sun had not yet reached it. When it did the heat of a Neapolitan summer lingering into September would quickly make a morning walk uncomfortable, but for a few minutes more the terraced gardens would be in cool shadow and Emma walked slowly down the winding drive. Cypress and azalea flanked it and between the shrubs and trees stood sculptured figures, fauns and nymphs and less readily identifiable lumps of stone retrieved from Herculaneum or Pompeii by her husband, whose antiquarian researches occupied much more of his time than his duties as British envoy. There was beauty in the shadowed garden, the tall cypresses dark against the dazzling blue of the sea, but Emma had no eyes for it. Her thoughts were of herself, her past and future.

It had been a tortuous road she had

travelled, first as Amy Hart, when she had been successively the mistress of Captain Payne and Sir Harry Fetherstonehaugh; then—when the Honourable Charles Greville had transferred her, for a consideration, to his uncle—Amy Lyon. And as Amy Lyon she had been married, after a few seasons, to her dear Sir William. Now she was Emma, Lady Hamilton, *persona grata* at the court of King Ferdinand of the Two Sicilies and bosom friend of Queen Maria Carolina, and that should be achievement enough for any aspiring woman of thirty-three. So she told herself. But she was not content. Sir William was kind, he let her do very much as she wanted, but he was after all thirty years older than she was and—to put it mildly —not very exciting. And now there was Nelson. It was four years since she had seen him, but she remembered that he certainly seemed *épris,* and she herself had found him attractive. Then he had been captain of the *Agamemnon* and now he was Rear-Admiral Sir Horatio; with only one arm, it was true, but he must be at least twenty years younger than Sir William—and a great hero, soon to be famous throughout the civilized world.

Two days ago the brig *Mutine* had brought the news of the Nile victory to Naples, eleven of the thirteen French battleships taken or destroyed, but it would take Nelson's battered ships many days, even weeks, to make their slow way along the Mediterranean to Naples. But then, oh, then, what celebrations there should be! Emma's dark-blue eyes shone with anticipation of those celebrations. Banquets, illuminations, balls, fireworks, and not just for one day but for many days. Her beloved Maria Carolina would easily persuade the King to throw open the palace for a week of feasting, and since Sir William disliked such junketings she, the ambassadress, would play a principal part. Emma was visualizing herself enthroned beside the one-armed admiral at a table laden with wines and rich confections, when her imaginings were cut short by the sound of noisy altercation not far ahead.

A final curve of the carriage-drive had brought her in sight of the lodge, a small building in the classical style to Sir William's own design, which stood to the left of the tall wrought-iron gates. Pozzi, the fat lodge-keeper, was standing on the inner side of the closed gates arguing with a man who stood outside. They were not near enough for words to be distinguished, but the furious dismissive gestures that accompanied Pozzi's shrill tones made it clear that some undesirable was being sent about his business. Emma, who knew Pozzi's over-officiousness, quickened her step. She was a dozen paces from the gates when the man outside threw up his hands as if in despair, turned, and was gone.

'What is this, Pozzi?' she demanded as she reached him.

'Ah, miladi, your pardon!' The lodge-keeper, who was in his shirtsleeves, contrived to bow while he hastily buttoned his breeches. 'Some *briccone,* some rascal come up from the port. A beggar, I think. *Per Dio!* The impudence of these dogs—'

'You think? What did he say?'

'Miladi, he spoke mostly in some foreign tongue. I made out only that he must see the British Envoy—those words he said in English—and would give his message to no one else. Without doubt he was—'

'Open the gate, and quickly!'

Emma snapped the words at him. Pozzi dragged the heavy gate open and she slipped out. The unfenced road that

14

wound down the bare hillsides to the upper streets of Naples ran almost level before dipping on the first of its many lacets and the dismissed visitor was in sight a pistol-shot away. Lady Hamilton, whose musical voice had delighted many a Neapolitan salon, could shout like a fishwife when she wanted to, and she shouted now.

'You, there! Come back here!'

The man had evidently enough Italian to understand that. He stopped and turned, hesitated for a second or two, and began to retrace his steps. His peculiar gait no less than his loose canvas trousers stained with tar marked him for a seaman; a lean dark-faced man with a red kerchief binding his ragged black curls. He halted a few paces from Emma, eyeing her suspiciously.

'Well?' she said, smiling at him. 'You wish to speak to Sir William Hamilton. I am Lady Hamilton and you may tell me what it is.'

A blank stare of incomprehension answered her. Four years in Naples had given Emma, besides her fluent Italian, a working knowledge of the *lingua franca* of the Mediterranean seaboard, and she tried him with that.

'Where do you come from?'

He understood her. 'From Ciudadela, signora.'

'Minorca?'

'*Si*, signora.'

Fishing-boats from the Balearic islands sometimes put in at Naples despite the fact that they were Spanish possessions and Britain, at war with Spain, used Naples as a port of supply. But what, Emma wondered, could bring a Minorcan fisherman to the Palazzo Sessa?

'You have a message for Sir William Hamilton, you say?' she said.

The fisherman shook his head violently. 'For British envoy. Only for British envoy.'

A second before he spoke his hand had moved towards the bosom of his linen blouse and fallen again. She moved towards him, frowning.

'I don't believe you.'

'*E vero*, signora, *e vero!*'

'Show me, then.'

He fumbled in his blouse, pulled out a small packet, and held it up for her to see. With the swiftness of a striking serpent her hand shot out and twitched it from his grasp. As she stepped quickly back he lunged forward to recapture it, but she was beyond his reach and Pozzi, scowling fiercely, was beside her. The fisherman, with an inarticulate cry of rage and a brandishing of clenched fists, swung round and set off in the direction of Naples as fast as his long legs would carry him.

'A *bandito* if ever I saw one!' fulminated Pozzi. 'Your ladyship ought not to venture—'

'You may as well open the gates,' Emma cut him short. 'Captain Harvey will be coming up from the port for the Gibraltar dispatches before long.'

She began to walk slowly back along the carriage-drive, examining the filched packet as she went. It was a roll of oiled canvas tied with tarry string, with no label or address attached; someone, it seemed likely, had instructed the fisherman to deliver it to the British Envoy at Naples and to no one else. Lady Hamilton had more than her share of curiosity and she saw no reason to respect the privacy of an unaddressed package. She loosened the string and unrolled the canvas, which held a stained and crumpled paper. When she had straightened this out she could just decipher the words written in English in an angular scrawl. They were brief and

17

not very illuminating: *I fear I am suspect. I must be taken off earlier than arranged. Cala Roqua midnight September 14, 15, 16. The word is Gibraltar. 0.*

2

'One inch and seven-eighths at the shoulders, Mr Snape,' said Sir William Hamilton, withdrawing his calipers from the little clay figurine he held in his left hand. 'Probably from the Etruscan period—add that, if you please.'

'One inch and seven-eighths, probably Etruscan period,' repeated Mr Snape *sotto voce*, as his quill scratched laboriously in the folio manuscript-book that lay open on the desk before him. Sir William, at his adjacent table, set aside the clay figurine and picked up another object from the assemblage at his elbow, which had been collected from the ruins of Pompeii some weeks ago. He screwed a watchmaker's glass into his eye and scrutinized it closely, turning it between his long delicate fingers, his thin aristocratic face intent below the carefully curled white hair, while Mr Snape waited with quill poised.

18

They were in one of the smaller rooms of the Palazzo Sessa, some sixty feet square with its domed and frescoed ceiling thirty feet overhead and its walls lined with shelves of vases, cabinets of coins, and cases of lava and coral specimens. This was not Sir William's study, which was smaller and reached from it by a connecting door; his second secretary—his political secretary—was at work in there. Mr Snape, a small skinny man with a pointed red nose, was no more than an amanuensis, a cataloguer of the spoils of antiquity, but the fact that he was always regarded as first secretary reflected the envoy's preoccupation with Roman remains, which he considered (though he would never have admitted it) of more importance than the affairs of the British Government.

'A lion,' said Sir William now. 'A lion couchant, I believe we may say.' He applied the calipers. 'In length—'

He stopped and turned as the door to the entrance hall opened. Mr Snape rose, bowed, and sat down again.

'Good morning, my dear Pliny,' said Emma; it was her pet name for him, chosen because that particular Roman was known as the Elder Pliny. 'Am I not up early?'

She deposited a kiss on the top of his white head.

'Good morning, my dear Emma. You are indeed early.' Sir William looked up at her with a slight frown. 'Must you wear that thing? It scarcely becomes you.'

'My fillet?' She pulled it off and held it up on her forefinger. 'The first of many celebrations, Pliny. "Nelson and Victory" will be the toast of all the world soon.'

'Our last news of the admiral was that *Vanguard* was off the coast of Crete and had lost her foremast,' Sir William pointed out. 'He will not reach Naples for a week.'

'Then my fillet must be seen as a rehearsal. What language do they speak on Minorca, Pliny?'

'A dialect of Catalan, I believe. Why do you ask, my dear?'

'There was a man at the gate this morning, a Minorcan fisherman, I think. He had a message for you and I took it from him.' She held out the crumpled paper. 'I can't make head or tail of it.'

Sir William took the paper and peered frowningly at the scrawled words.

20

'"Must be taken off"—h'm—"word is Gibraltar"—and the "O", one presumes, should identify the sender.' He shook his head slowly. 'I cannot think this is for me. I can attach no—but stay! Minorca—I fancy there was something in dispatches last month—Mr Snape!'

Mr Snape bobbed up from his desk. 'Sir William?'

'We must interrupt our work for a moment. Pray ask Mr Torrens to join me here. He is to bring the Most Secret file.'

'Yes, Sir William.'

'And Mr Snape—take that catalogue to the study with you and check yesterday's entries. With the greatest care, of course.'

'Of course, Sir William.'

Mr Snape departed with the big book under his arm. Sir William studied the writing on the paper again.

'A scholarly hand were it less hastily penned,' he remarked.

'Perhaps a learned antiquarian like yourself, my love,' Emma suggested lightly. 'He's been caught trying to steal ancient Roman chamber-pots from Minorca.'

Her husband frowned. 'Those or any other Roman vessels are most unlikely to be found on Minorca, my dear Emma,' he said reprovingly. 'I am told there are megaliths, and though I have not myself seen them I would say that they must antedate the Roman era by many centuries. Since we have no written account of their origin—'

But Lady Hamilton had ceased to listen and was crossing the room towards a gilt-framed pier-glass on the opposite wall. As she reached it the second secretary came out of the study with a stiff-covered folder in his hand. He was a tall and elegantly dressed young man with a nose indubitably Roman, though he had no interest at all in the Rome of Sir William's ruling passion.

'Ah, Robert,' said the envoy with a welcoming smile. 'Put that thing on the desk and sit down.'

Mr Torrens had come out from England only six months ago, and Mr Snape had been at the Embassy for five years; but whereas Henry Snape was the third son of an obscure clergyman, Robert Torrens was the second son of an earl; while Sir William was a cousin of the Duke of Hamilton. Thus it was naturally 'Robert' for the second secretary and a punctilious 'Mr Snape' for the first.

'We have here a little mystery, Robert,'

the Envoy said, handing him the creased note. 'A Minorcan fisherman brought it this morning.'

The secretary studied the note with care.

'It has reminded me of something,' Sir William continued. 'Did we not last month receive from Gibraltar a Most Secret concerning Minorca? The copy of an Admiralty directive, I seem to remember—'

'I know, sir,' Torrens cut in without ceremony. 'The memorandum about Oliviera.'

'You always know, Robert,' said Sir William with a touch of envy.

Knowledge was Mr Torrens's speciality. He seemed to know everyone and everything, except matters concerning ancient Rome. He ruffled quickly through the papers in the folder, selected one, and handed it to the envoy.

'Delivered with C-in-C's dispatches 10th August, sir,' he said briskly. 'Brought by *Perseverance*, 18–gun brig-sloop, Captain Holbrook.'

Sir William scanned the document, holding it in one hand while the other toyed with the little model of a couchant lion. It was written in a clerkly script and the words 'For your information, no action needed' had been added at the foot by some other writer. The heading MOST SECRET, balanced by the address of the Admiralty in Whitehall in the opposite corner, prefaced a considerable screed:

To the Right Honourable Lord St Vincent, Commander in Chief of His Majesty's Ships and Vessels employed and to be employed in the Mediterranean etc. etc. etc.

Whereas the Bearer of this letter, Doctor Miguel Oliviera, is in the Service of Their Lordships, you are hereby required and directed to land the said Doctor Miguel Oliviera at some suitable place on the coast of the Island of Minorca secretly and by night and to effect this without the least delay, selecting therefor a vessel suited to the nature of the operation. A place and time and date for taking off the said Doctor Miguel Oliviera from the Isle of Minorca will be arranged by him and you are directed to provide a vessel accordingly.

24

And for so doing this shall be your Order.

Given by the Board of Admirals this 7th day of July 1798.

Two indecipherable signatures followed. Sir William looked up from his perusal.

'Who is this Doctor Miguel Oliviera?' he asked, wrinkling his brow. 'Do you know of him, Robert?'

'I've heard of him, sir. A Portuguese, supposed to be an antiquary, a dedicated enemy to Spain.'

'It seems to me to be possible, even probable, that the "O" of this morning's missive is this Oliviera. Would you agree?'

'It's plain enough.' Torrens, as usual, had the air of concealing his contempt for lesser intelligences. 'Oliviera was landed, no doubt to assume the character of a visiting Spanish antiquary—he could pass for a Spaniard—and the date for taking him off was arranged. Now he fears his disguise is penetrated and wants to get clear.'

'Then he should have sent his appeal for help to St Vincent at Gibraltar,' Sir William said. 'I have no powers from Admiralty.'

'Consider, sir. Minorca is enemy territory. No vessels thence would put in to Gibraltar.'

'Then I must send Oliviera's message to Gibraltar. The vessel with my dispatches leaves this evening.'

'But Pliny—this is urgent, surely.' Emma, who had been adjusting her fillet in front of the pier-glass, had come to stand beside them. 'I think you should act quickly.'

'Lady Hamilton is right, sir,' Torrens said. 'A fast-sailing craft with fair winds might make the passage from Minorca in six days and today is the 10th. If Oliviera sent off his message on the 3rd that's a week ago, and if he's to be taken off when he asks we've barely time to get a ship to the Minorcan coast—where, one assumes, this Cala Roqua he mentions is located.'

'God bless my soul!' Sir William passed both hands over his white curls. 'What ships have I? Why am I to be pestered with the affairs of agents, spies—for, I take it, Oliviera is a spy. Why is he in Minorca? Tell me that, Robert.'

Emma smiled at the second secretary. 'Oh, Mr Torrens will know for sure. What he don't know isn't knowledge.'

'Thank you, Lady Hamilton,' Torrens

said stiffly. 'As it chances, I'm aware that an early invasion of Minorca is contemplated, the object of course being the securing of Port Mahon as a naval base. Oliviera will have been sent to obtain information of fortifications and batteries, locations of troops, warships in harbour—that kind of thing. It's rumoured that General Stuart is to command the invasion force,' he added.

'Charles Stuart? I knew his father. But—may I ask—how do you come by these tidings, Robert?'

'A letter from my brother, sir, by the last mail. As you know, he is secretary to the Second Lord.'

'It appears to me,' said Sir William drily, 'that the words "most secret" are scarcely an apt description of this affair. Well, I suppose we must—' He interrupted himself. 'What is it, my dear?'

'Carriage wheels,' Emma said; she went to the window and looked out. 'It's Captain Harvey—he looks more like a boiled lobster than ever.'

'Oblige me by not making fun of Harvey, Emma. He's a good man—and comes most opportunely. The dispatches are ready, Robert?'

'Ready and sealed, sir.'

'Bring them, if you please. Emma, my love, have you no occupation elsewhere?'

Emma pouted. 'I want to stay, Pliny, and hear what's to happen with my Minorca message. I swear I'll not laugh at Harvey.'

'Oh, very well then. Please to bring that chair nearer the table.'

An olive-skinned footman in livery entered and stood by the door to announce the visitor.

'The Capitan Harr-vay, your excellency.'

Harvey gave his cocked hat to the footman as he rolled in, a corpulent redfaced man not undeserving of Emma's vulgar description. He shook the open flaps of his gold-epauletted blue coat as he crossed the room to make his bow.

'Servant, my lady. 'Nother hot one, Sir William.' He sat down heavily at Sir William's gesture and cleared his throat. 'Confound the dust! I'm as hoarse as a crow, not to say as hot as a roast turkey.'

'Cheer up, captain,' Emma said. 'The *tramontana* will cool you.'

'Yes, but it don't blow until sundown, and I've to sweat—begging your pardon

28

—until then. A man of my build don't take kindly to heat no matter how long he's been used to it. 'Morning, Mr Torrens.'

Torrens, who had come from the study, returned the greeting as he placed a thin canvas-covered packet on the table.

'Thank you, Robert. That will be all, I think,' Sir William added as the secretary paused, waiting.

Mr Torrens was plainly doubtful whether the envoy was capable of dealing with the Oliviera business without a secretary's help, but he dutifully retired to the study.

'The dispatches are here, captain,' Sir William said, tapping the packet, 'but you'll stay to take lunch with us, I hope?'

'Not I, with thanks to your excellency. Last news from the Fleet is that *Culloden*'s going to need new bottom-planking when she comes in and I've to get this lead-bellied dockyard moving—I wish to God we had our own dockyard here.' The captain mopped his shining face with a large silk handkerchief. 'I'll see the dispatches on board myself as usual. Gib's sent a 12–gun cutter this time. *Snipe*'s her name.'

'Is she a small vessel with one tall mast?' Emma asked suddenly.

29

'She is, my lady. Lying off the Mola Figlio.'

'Then I've a bone to pick with you, captain. Last evening—my dear Maria Carolina told me this—last evening some of the Queen's ladies-in-waiting were in a state barge with the Marquis of Ariano, taking a pleasure-cruise round the harbour, and when they came near this Royal Navy ship they called out to say they were coming on board. The captain was on deck and he shouted at them to sheer off. And when they called again—he must be a perfect savage, this captain—he positively bellowed at them that no women were allowed on board his ship. Women!' She shook her head at him reprovingly. 'That's not like the British Navy, captain.'

Captain Harvey looked a trifle uncomfortable. 'Pray accept my 'pologies, Lady Hamilton. I'll take order with Mr Saville when I see him.'

Sir William, who had been drumming impatiently with his fingers on the table, stopped it and looked up.

'Is that John Saville, of the Norfolk Savilles?'

'That's the man,' Harvey nodded.

30

'Do you know him, Pliny?' demanded Emma.

Sir William shook his head. 'I knew that he had a naval command, and I know his story. He was engaged to be married to Lady Flora Caldecot and she jilted him—ran away with her footman. She treated him monstrously. That may not excuse his behaviour but it may explain it.'

'Then he's a misogynist, I suppose,' Emma said scornfully.

Her husband looked at her with some surprise. 'May I ask where you learned that word, my dear?'

'It was in *Clarissa* and I looked it up.'

'Oh—Richardson's novel. But we have a less fictitious matter to deal with, captain, and I ask your help in it.' Sir William handed over Oliviera's note and the Admiralty directive. 'The message reached me this morning. We believe it to be directly linked to the directive addressed to the Commander-in-Chief. It seems to us—to me, that is—that this man Oliviera, an agent of Mr Pitt's, no doubt, should have his request to be taken off from Minorca acted upon, and that without delay. I understand that the information

31

Oliviera may have gathered may be of the first importance in a proposed invasion of Minorca.'

Harvey looked up from his reading. 'They're going to take Mahon at last? Thank God they've seen the light. The harbour and dockyard will be worth a mountain of gold to the Navy. And you're right about Oliviera, Sir William. We'll have to get the feller off somehow. Trouble is there's only one British vessel in harbour and that's *Snipe*.'

'We could use her?'

'We'll have to. She's short-handed, too —first lieutenant ashore in hospital—in hospital here, God help him!—with malignant fever. I'm sending a passenger for Gib on board this evening, though, and he can stand a watch.' He broke off to indulge a fit of coughing. 'The trouble is *Snipe*'s orders. Saville's orders are to carry your dispatches to Gib and evade any action with the enemy. Send her to Gib by way of Minorca and she's into enemy waters. The Dons won't have any 74s in Mahon now but they'll have other craft—' again the cough interrupted him. 'Your pardon—throat's as dry as a cook's oven.'

'It's for me to ask pardon,' Sir William said. 'I should have offered you a drink on your arrival. Emma, my dear—'

'I'll get it myself.' She stood up. 'What's Captain Harvey's fancy?'

'If it could be lemon-water with a spice of brandy, my lady—'

'It could. And I'm glad you're sending *Snipe* for the Oliviera man. I feel responsible for him. After all, it was me who started it all.'

'It was I, my dear,' Sir William corrected her.

'No, it wasn't, Pliny. You'd never have heard of Oliviera's troubles if it hadn't been for me.'

Lady Hamilton went out through the big door leading to the hall. Captain Harvey leaned across the table, his red face creased in a frown.

'You must understand this, Sir William,' he said, 'I'll need your authority. I can draft an order for Saville, instructions to take off Oliviera and the password and so forth, but in doing so I'm countermanding—or at least amending—C-in-C's order. An authorization from you, in writing—'

'I have no naval authority whatever,' objected the envoy quickly.

'You're the only British authority there is in these parts, sir, and I've my career to consider. They'd not relieve you of your post for authorizing an urgent mission.'

'But—oh, very well, then.'

Sir William, with no very good grace, shifted himself to the desk and took a sheet of paper from its drawer.

'By the bye,' he said as he picked up Mr Snape's quill. 'This Cala Roqua, where Oliviera appoints the rendezvous—have you any notion where it is?'

'None, save that it's likely to be near Ciudadela if the fisherman that brought the message came from there. *Snipe* will have to find it.'

3

Captain Harvey's position at Naples was an anomalous one: he had no official existence. In this fifth year of the war Naples was a neutral port, debarred from rendering any assistance to the armed forces of either side; and with the kingdom of Naples and the Two Sicilies threatened from the north by the advancing Republican armies King

Ferdinand was sitting uneasily on the fence, waiting to come down on the side that showed certainty of victory. So as port officer for the British Navy, which in effect he was, Captain Harvey had no admitted existence, no official powers, a minimal staff as non-existent as himself, and a difficult job to perform. He was very well supplied with British gold, however, which served admirably to relax the bonds of neutrality in the shipyards of Naples, besides enabling him to keep a respectable mistress in a villa halfway up the hill.

Harvey was a kindly man and disliked giving pain to man or beast. On the long and mildly hazardous drive down to Naples from the Palazzo Sessa, he had been considering the matter of the reprimand he was bound to give *Snipe*'s captain for his rudeness to the Queen's friends. In the ordinary way he would have taken a boat out to *Snipe* and delivered Sir William's dispatches to Saville himself, but the reprimand that had to be given at the same time made this inadvisable; in a small vessel like the cutter there was no privacy, and Harvey was not the man to give a commanding officer a dressing-down in the hearing of his crew. He would send a boat to bring Saville ashore, he decided, and deal with him in the port office.

The *carrozza* set him down at the gates of the quays and he walked in, threading a noisy crowd of beggars and stevedores and dodging carts and barrows, and sweating mightily under the inexorable sun. His office consisted of two small rooms on the ground floor of a warehouse, with no exterior sign of its identity except a seaman in a straw hat and white smock—one of his three naval ratings—who stood on guard at its door. The man stood to attention and doffed his hat as the captain came up.

'Captain of *Snipe*'s reported 'ere ten minutes ago, sir,' he said. ''E's waitin' in your cabin.'

'Very well, Padgett. Get along to the yard and see those idle dogs are getting on with *Vanguard*'s foremast.'

'Aye aye, sir.'

Harvey went in and through to his inner room, which was plainly furnished with a table, two chairs, and a cupboard. The officer who was standing at the grimy window turned and took off his cocked hat. He was a big man in blue coat and white breeches, the coat gold-braided on cuffs and lapels but lacking epaulettes, indicating that he was a Royal Navy lieutenant.

''Morning, Mr Saville,' Harvey said. 'Didn't expect you ashore so early.'

'Good morning, sir. I've been visiting my lieutenant, Mr Sims, in hospital.'

Saville's voice was a deep growl. He had a large head and its clustered black curls were tinged with grey above the ears. But for the sullen droop at the corners of an obstinate-looking mouth his dark angular face might have been called handsome.

'Oh, ah.' Harvey mopped sweat from his face and neck. 'How's he doing?'

'Badly. A high fever. I'm told he can't be moved and I'll have to sail without him. He seems to be well cared for there.'

'Sisters of the Annunciation, ain't it? I'll look in on him in a day or two.'

The captain replaced his hat, which he had removed to wipe his brow, and sat down at the table, his rubicund features contorting themselves into a scowl.

'Now, Mr Saville, let's get this over. It's been reported to me that last evening you behaved with marked discourtesy to some ladies of the Queen's court. Is that so?'

Saville had been standing with his wide shoulders hunched and a slight forward

37

stoop, an attitude not unusual with tall officers accustomed to the low deckheads in His Majesty's ships. Now he straightened himself and brought his heels together.

'I told a barge to keep clear of my ship, sir,' he said stiffly.

'My informant says you told 'em to sheer off and called 'em women.'

'Women they were, sir, by your leave. I wouldn't call a woman of Maria Carolina's court a lady.'

Captain Harvey was much of the same opinion, but he forced himself to speak severely.

'That's beside the point, Mr Saville. The point is that it's presently vital to the Navy's interest to preserve friendly relations with the Neapolitans. Especially with the Queen. Maria has Ferdinand under her thumb, as you may know. As I understand, these—these females asked if they might come aboard—'

'Sir, as *Snipe*'s captain—'

'I know, I know. You allow no women on board your ship. Very well. I'm ordering you, Mr Saville, to speak 'em fair when you're in this harbour. You'll see to it, if you please.'

'Aye aye, sir,' Saville growled.

'Very well and that's that.' Captain Harvey blew out his breath, took off his hat, and swabbed his face again. 'Dispatches for Gib.' He laid a packet on the table. 'And I've further orders for you. Sit down. You'll sail before sunset?' he added as the lieutenant obeyed.

'As soon as the *tramontana* gives me a wind, sir.'

'And you'll be heading sou'west instead of north-west. *Snipe*'s to return to Gib by way of the Balearics. Far as distance is concerned you'll have a shorter voyage, rounding Cape Spartivento, but—as I don't need to tell you—you'll be in Spanish waters when you reach Minorca.'

Saville's craggy face had not altered its set expression while the captain was administering his reprimand, but now he frowned and shot a quick glance at his senior.

'This order comes from C-in-C, sir?' he said abruptly.

'No. From the envoy. His Excellency takes full responsibility.' Harvey had taken two papers from his pocket; he pushed the larger sheet across the table. 'Read that. It sets forth your orders in full, as far as they go.'

Saville read the paper slowly, his heavy black brows drawn together. Harvey waited impatiently and then passed across the second paper, the crumpled message from Miguel Oliviera.

'That's what set the ball rolling,' he said. 'It reached Sir William two hours ago, brought by a fishing-boat out of Ciudadela.'

Saville read the envoy's orders a second time before picking up Oliviera's note and giving it a long scrutiny.

'Well?' Harvey demanded. 'You understand what you're to do, Mr Saville?'

'I believe so, sir.' The lieutenant's deep voice was expressionless. 'I am to take my ship to Minorca and there find an inlet or cove named Cala Roqua, said to be probably in the neighbourhood of Ciudadela. I am to land a boat there at midnight on 14 September and take off a man named Oliviera. The password by which we identify each other is "Gibraltar". If the man is not there I am to land a boat on the 15th and if that fails on the 16th. It's not impossible that Oliviera will have been taken by the Spaniards before I reach Minorca, in which case I shall have remained off an enemy coast for three days to no purpose. Finally, I sail for Gibraltar, with or without Oliviera, on the 17th.'

'Just so.' The captain eyed him askance. 'From your manner of putting it, Mr Saville, a man might think you disliked those orders.'

'I believe I know my duty, sir. I don't question my orders. I must point out, however, that the time allowed me for finding this rendezvous is short, and that I have no chart of the Minorcan coast.'

'You have the general chart.'

'I have, sir. As you know, it doesn't mark the names of minor inlets.'

'Then you'll have to waylay a local fishing-boat and ask,' Harvey said. 'I think you make difficulties, Mr Saville,' he added irritably.

A spark of anger flashed in Saville's eyes.

'By your leave, sir,' he growled, 'I don't make them. I call your attention to them. Naturally I shall carry out my orders to the best of my ability.'

'Glad to hear it,' said the captain with faint irony. 'For not doing that on his Minorcan expedition in '56 Admiral Byng was court-martialled and shot.'

This doubtful jest seemed to restore his

amiability, though it brought no answering smile from Saville. Harvey ran a finger round inside his stock and sat back in his chair.

'It may be a queer mission, Mr Saville,' he said, 'but by God I envy you! I'd give a month's pay to get to sea again. Any more questions?'

'One further point, sir. With Sims ashore I'm short of a watchkeeping officer. Midshipman Hope is not qualified—'

'Belay there.' Captain Harvey sat up suddenly. 'Damned if I hadn't forgotten. You're carrying a passenger to Gib, survivor from *Courier*.' He took a watch from the pocket of his white waistcoat and glanced at it. 'Told him to be down on the Vittoria quay at four bells—he should be there in half an hour. Rated master's mate, so he can stand watches for you.'

'I'll send *Snipe*'s boat for him in half an hour, then.' Saville put dispatches and papers in his pocket and stood up. 'The man's name, sir?'

'Eh? Oh—Mitton, was it? No—Fitton, that's it. Michael Fitton.'

2   Ship's Company

1

Michael Fitton fell in love with *Snipe* at
first sight.

She was lying at moorings a cable-length
off the Mola Figlio, and as the boat
pulled clear of the fishing-smacks and
coasting brigs crowded along the quayside
she came into his view, a thoroughbred
among cart-horses. No breath of wind
ruffled the waters of the harbour, and the
single tall mast bare of crosstrees, the six
black-painted gunports in the white band
that ran the length of her side, the slender
bowsprit nearly half as long as the hull,
were all duplicated in perfect reflection.
He was familiar with armed cutters and
had served in one, *Curlew*, for a short
period, but there was a difference with
this one. She was, he thought, rather larger
than *Curlew*, or at least longer in the hull,
and had a more graceful sheer to her bows.

She had wheel steering instead of a tiller, too. To Mr Fitton's experienced eye her lines and rigging hinted that here was a prime sailer, a good sea-boat; but it was the sheer beauty of her as she rested lightly on her inverted image that won his heart at a glance.

Snipe's boat, which had picked him up from the Vittoria quay, was little bigger than a cockboat and was pulled by two seamen, youngish men in clean white blouses and loose much-patched trousers. Mr Fitton sat in the sternsheets beside the midshipman at the tiller, a gangling youth of sixteen or seventeen whose snub-nosed face seemed set in an expression of surprise and whose cocked hat was a size too big for him. Apart from an initial shout to know whether he was the passenger for *Snipe* the midshipman had not spoken to him, possibly because he was naturally shy or—more probably—because he didn't know what to make of a man in worn naval rig and battered hat who hadn't so much as a bag with him by way of dunnage.

Mr Fitton, never a talkative man, was not sorry to be silent. He liked to savour the moments of change and new prospect in life and this was, for him, such a moment. Not that the prospect of being landed at Gibraltar to be mewed up in the naval barracks and await drafting appealed to him; but he was going to sea again, he would have a deck under his feet once more if only for the five or six days it would take *Snipe* to reach Gibraltar, and after the tedious wait in squalid lodgings ashore that would be very heaven. His five fellow-survivors from the ill-fated *Courier* had left Naples some days earlier, and though his Stoic philosophy inclined him to self-sufficiency he looked forward to making one of a ship's company, for he could be sure that duties would be found for a master's mate.

'Boat ahoy! What boat's that?'

The hail was prescriptive, even when it was perfectly obvious that this was *Snipe*'s boat and midshipman at a distance of a hundred fathoms. The midshipman duly returned the hail in his high tenor voice.

'Passenger for *Snipe!*'

The man who had hailed from *Snipe*'s deck disappeared and the boat continued to pull in towards her side. The midshipman turned to his passenger.

'He'll tell the captain,' he said, 'but I'll—hup!—announce you myself when we

45

get aboard.' He seemed to be afflicted with hiccups. 'Hup!—sir,' he added uncertainly.

Probably the 'sir' came out because Mr Fitton had the look of a man accustomed to command; his rating of master's mate made him only a half-step senior in rank though he was at least a dozen years older than the midshipman.

He nodded. 'Very well, Mr—'

'Hope, sir, Henry Hope. Way enough! Bows!'

The boat sheered neatly alongside and the bowman drew her in with his boathook. The cutter's freeboard was less than seven feet and Mr Fitton swung himself inboard with a toehold on the sill of a gunport. The seaman on deck-watch, back at his post, stood stiffly at attention, a fresh-faced man of thirty or so whose wide mouth and somewhat protuberant ears seemed vaguely familiar.

'Stand by for a jiffy.' Midshipman Hope landed on the deck as he touched his hat to a non-existent quarterdeck. 'I'll tell him you've come aboard.'

He ran to the open hatch on the after-deck and disappeared down it, leaving Mr Fitton to glance round him with a critical eye: a spotless deck, falls coiled-down to perfection, a dozen off-duty seamen chatting and laughing up in the bows, a party making some adjustment to the side-tackles of the starboard 12–pounders under the direction of a skinny little man who was probably the gunner. He liked what he saw, but had only time for a quick look before Mr Hope bobbed up on deck again.

'You're to report,' he said, jerking his thumb backwards.

The hatch gave on to a short ladder-way, and descending this Mr Fitton was confronted by the narrow open door of a cabin little more than seven feet square, lit fairly adequately by the sunlight that streamed through a scuttle in the low deckhead. A large man of about his own age sat at a very small table with a muster-book open before him and man and table seemed to fill the cabin. He put his battered hat under his arm and ducked inside.

'Reporting on board, sir. Michael Fitton, master's mate.'

Snipe's captain, directing a steady stare at him from beneath lowered brows, saw a square-built man of middle height whose brown face seemed to have been carved from a block of teak; his white breeches, though as clean as scrubbing could make them, were patched and mended in half-a-dozen places and his coat, more rusty-green than blue, was stained and threadbare.

'How long have you served in the Royal Navy, Mr Fitton?' he demanded harshly.

'Eighteen years, sir.'

'Then you should know better than to board one of His Majesty's ships looking like a damned scarecrow.'

Since this seemed to call for no reply Mr Fitton remained silent, his face totally expressionless. There was a pause while Saville Wrote in the muster-book and when he spoke it was without looking up.

'Your last ship was *Courier*. She was sunk off Malta. When?'

'Ninth of June, sir.'

'Today is the eighth of September. You've not been ashore at Naples for three months, Mr Fitton.'

'No, sir.'

'Where, then?'

'Malta and Sicily, sir.'

'You landed on Malta? It was occupied by the French?'

'Yes, sir.'

Saville sat back in his chair and glared

at him. 'I take it you can say more than "yes, sir" and "no, sir", Mr Fitton,' he said acidly. 'I'll thank you for a connected account of your doings from the sinking of *Courier* to your arrival in Naples.'

Mr Fitton, slightly disconcerted, blinked. He could have filled a book with the hazards and misadventures of that eventful time, but unlike most seamen he disliked spinning yarns. He decided to cut this one as short as he could.

'Aye aye, sir,' he said impassively. 'After *Courier*'s sinking I was in charge of the longboat with fifteen survivors. We succeeded in making Malta, fifty miles, and lost six men in a skirmish with the French. The rest of us were hidden and fed by friendly Maltese. After some days we succeeded in capturing a small brig and sailed for Naples. Some of the crew mutinied and myself with five men were turned adrift.'

'Where?' Saville demanded.

'Ten miles off the Sicilian coast, sir, in fair weather. We landed and made our way overland to Syracuse. At a place on the way we were arrested as vagrants and held in jail for a week. It was another three weeks before we could find a ship to take us from Syracuse to Naples.'

When he had finished speaking Saville was silent for some moments. When he spoke it was without emphasis.

'You'll please to consider my comment on your appearance unsaid, Mr Fitton. My lieutenant Mr Sims is in hospital and Mr Hope is not qualified to stand a watch,' he went on in the same tone. 'I'm ordered to land you at Gibraltar. You'll stand watch-and-watch with me on the voyage.'

'Aye aye, sir.'

'You'll take over Mr Sims's cabin, aft here starboard side. You'll mess—' the brief hesitation was almost unnoticeable—'with Mr Hope and the warrant officers. I shall sail at sunset. You've served in cutters?'

'I was in *Curlew,* sir, for three months.'

'Very well.' Saville fixed a frowning stare on his new deck-officer. 'Mr Hope will acquaint you with my standing orders but there's one you'll pay particular attention to, Mr Fitton. No craft with a woman on board is to come closer than hailing-distance to this vessel. In no circumstances are women allowed to board my ship. You understand?'

'Yes, sir.'

'Then you'd best make yourself familiar

with *Snipe.*' He raised his voice in a thunderous shout. 'Mr Hope!'

A faint reply came from on deck, and the midshipman clattered down the ladderway to doff his hat and squeeze into the cabin.

'Take Mr Fitton round the ship, Mr Hope,' Saville said peremptorily.

'Aye aye, sir. Sir—by your leave, sir—' Mr Hope, embarrassed, darted a sidelong glance at his fellow-officer. 'Do I call him—hup!—I mean, do I address Mr Fitton as "sir"?'

'Certainly you do, Mr Hope,' Saville rapped. 'Until we reach Gibraltar Mr Fitton will act as my first lieutenant.'

'Aye aye, sir. After you, sir,' he added as he and the temporarily promoted master's mate withdrew from the cabin.

They came up into the heat and dazzle of the deck within a few paces of the seaman on gangway duty, and once again Mr Fitton was assailed by a sense of familiarity. Perhaps the man had served in the same ship with him. He halted as the man turned to face him and touched his broad-brimmed straw hat.

'What's your name?' he asked.

'Dancer, sir.' The seaman grinned

51

uncertainly. 'Born an' bred up in Gleadsmoss, sir—'tis nobbut five mile from Gawsworth.'

The mists of nearly twenty years lifted and Mr Fitton saw again the grey pile of Gawsworth Hall, once the home of the Fittons; the lodge where he and his widowed mother had lived, dispossessed and impoverished; and the lad who came twice a week to dig his mother's garden.

'George Dancer!' he exclaimed, and held out his hand.

The seaman grasped it. 'That same, sir. An' happy to see you aboard us.'

'An old shipmate, sir?' asked the midshipman as they walked on.

'No. Neighbours in Cheshire many years ago.'

'Oh. I'm a Berkshire man myself, sir. Shall we take the upper deck first, or start below?'

'As you will, Mr Hope. No other guide I seek. Milton.'

'Milton, sir? My father's rector of Milton.'

'It was the poet Milton I referred to,' Mr Fitton said without a smile. 'Shall we begin by this aftermost 12–pounder and proceed clockwise?'

2

HMS Snipe was one of the smallest of the unrated small vessels in the Service; a lieutenant's command, with a junior lieutenant and a midshipman to second him. Her crew of 38 seamen, a cook, and 3 warrant officers, her length of 64 feet and her 24–foot beam, made her as different from a 74–gun battleship as a rustic hamlet is different from a teeming city. Here was a little community that was all seamen—no marines, no chaplain, no surgeons, no master-at-arms or captain's secretaries—living at very close quarters, each man's life depending for comfort on the goodfellowship of his mates; in a mess-deck where the allowance for slinging hammocks is 14 inches per man there is no place for the unsociable or bad-tempered. Mr Fitton, aware of all this, was also aware that lack of the rigid routine and merciless discipline of a 74 could render a cutter's crew slack and slovenly. But as he progressed on his tour with Midshipman Hope he quickly perceived that this was not so with *Snipe*.

'We reeved new breechings coming up from Gib,' Hope was saying as they walked for'ard along the port side, past the 12–pounders bowsed-up tight against their closed gunports. 'We haven't fired a gun in action since we've been in the Med—and that don't please Mr Adey, the gunner. That's him, with the working-party t'other side.'

'Where was *Snipe* before you came out?'

'Channel patrol until November. The nearest we—hup!—got to action then was firing across the bows of smuggling craft. The Old—the captain was hoping we'd meet a Frog privateer, but no such—'

Hope halted suddenly to stare at his companion with his mouth open.

'What is it?' asked Mr Fitton.

'Begging your pardon, sir, but—but are you the Fitton that sank Dorimond's *Vengeur* off the Brittany coast in May '96?'

'I didn't sink *Vengeur*, Mr Hope. Captain Dorimond chose to follow my captured brig across a dangerous shoal, and she struck. She was lost with all hands.'

'They were still talking about it at Portsmouth when we put in there,' said Hope, still staring.

'They must be short of news in Portsmouth,' Mr Fitton remarked, starting to walk on. '*Snipe* hoists three jibs, I take it?'

The midshipman accepted this change of subject with evident disappointment but made haste to answer.

'Yes, sir—thirty-foot bowsprit and the outer spar is re—hup!—retractable!' He pronounced the word with some pride. 'Gives us eighteen feet without the jib-boom, for rough weather. Sixty feet with the topmast,' he added, jerking a thumb upwards as they passed the foot of the mast. 'We set a square-sail when the wind's abaft the beam; and by thunder, sir, you should see her fly—but of course you will—with a beam wind! I'll take my oath there's not a vessel afloat that could match her.'

'And your cook matches your ship, I trust.'

They had come abreast of the galley chimney, just for'ard of the mast; its black stove-pipe had a broad rim of brass, and the brass was as bright as elbow-grease could make it.

'Oh, Joe Dung's a paradox.' It was to be assumed that Hope meant 'paragon'.

'Dung's his native name, sir—he comes from Malacca or somewhere—but he's a wizard with duff.'

The group of seamen in the bows stopped talking as they approached, and the men who had been lounging against the rail or squatting on the deck stood up. Mr Fitton hesitated. The midshipman showed no sign of explaining his presence on board; an explanation, he thought, which should have come from Saville. He had better do it himself.

'Good morning, all,' he said cheerfully. 'I'm Fitton, master's mate, taking passage with you for Gib. Captain Saville has appointed me watchkeeping officer so you'll see more of me.'

They were a keen-looking lot, he noted, most of them young, with three older seamen sporting the short tarred pigtails that betokened old man-of-war's men. The gunner and his party had come for'ard while he was speaking, and now they were joined by a heavily-built man of middle age who emerged on deck from the fore-hatch. Mr Hope, suddenly aware of his responsibilities, performed introductions and Mr Fitton shook hands with Mr Knott the boatswain and Mr Adey the gunner.

'You've a trim vessel here, Mr Knott,' he said.

The boatswain, whose sharp grey eyes had been surveying him critically, looked pleased but wagged his head. 'She's well enough, Mr Fitton, well enough. Not as I could wish, though, and for why? Because she's undermanned.'

'Six hands in horspital at Gib,' supplemented Mr Adey, thrusting forward his beak of a nose and wrinkled yellow face; he was older than Knott, with wispy grey hair. 'We've not enough to man both broadsides, and she'd be a deal better with four-pounder long guns 'stead of these dommed carronades.'

'She's well enough as she is, Mr Adey,' Knott said reprovingly.

The gunner snorted. 'She'll not be well enough long, then. The for'ard ringbolt on number eight's tackle is nigh on drawing from the wood. You'd better see it.'

With a nod to their new shipmate they moved away towards the starboard guns.

'Take a look below now, sir?' Hope said.

'Lead on,' said Mr Fitton.

They descended the ladder-way of the fore-hatch into a gloom that was welcome

57

after the brassy glare on deck, but in spite of all four hatches being open to give ventilation it was hot and stuffy under the low deckheads. Here, right up in the bows, were steward's room and carpenter's and boatswain's storerooms, where the cable-locker would have been in a larger ship; the cables were stowed on long racks on either side. Ducking through a narrow doorway they found Joe Dung in his tiny galley, burnishing a saucepan and apparently oblivious of the heat, for his grinning liver-coloured face and completely bald head showed no glisten of sweat.

'Mr Fitton here is a judge of duff, Joe,' Hope told him. 'You'll show him you're a dab hand in that line, eh?'

'Dot's right, sah,' said Joe, bobbing his hairless dome vigorously.

Immediately aft of the galley the butt of the mast came down through the deck, as thick as a well-grown tree, to vanish below the planking to its rest on the keelson. Beyond it was the sail-room, a model of orderliness, and then the comparative roominess of the messdeck, no less than twelve feet wide and giving space for two narrow tables with benches by them on which men were sitting, some sewing or doing scrimshank work on bits of bone or wood and others talking. The buzz of conversation stopped as the two officers came in and the men stood up. Mr Fitton saw no reason to repeat his self-introduction, which he had found embarrassing, and they passed through quickly; but he had time to note the exactness with which the hammocks were ranged in their wooden nettings on either hand and the precision that had resulted in the mugs hung in a row on the bulk head being all at the same angle.

The ladder to the main hatch, wide enough for two men abreast, brought them up to the deck amidships. Mr Fitton, blinking in the brilliant light, saw that a boat was just pulling away from the cutter's side towards the quay and that Saville was standing at the after rail scowling at a letter in his hand. Then he was following Hope down a narrower ladder-way into near-darkness again.

'Gunner's quarters,' Hope said. 'Mind your head, sir.'

It was a good job that Mr Adey was so small a man. His filling-room, light-room and magazine were all got into a space of some thirty square feet, and his berth, a mere shelf, opened in the bulkhead of the magazine. His store-room with its neatly stacked sponge-and-rammers, water buckets and coils of slow-match was no bigger than the broom-cupboard in Mr Fitton's old home. Not for the first time, he admired the ingenuity that had converted every available inch of space into a storage place or a berth. There was a berth in the outboard bulkhead of the little cabin on the port side into which the midshipman now led him, which was barely large enough for a table and benches that might seat six men sitting very close together.

'You'll mess with the captain, I suppose, sir,' Hope said interrogatively.

'No. With the warrant officers.'

'Oh. Then you'll mess in here, same as me. Aft of this there's only the captain's quarters and the bread-room. If you're to berth in Mr Sims's cabin you come at it by the captain's ladder-way and go to starboard at the bottom—'

He stopped speaking as the green curtain covering the opening of the berth was pulled back and a head poked out, a head not much unlike that of an elderly sheep.

'Mr Owen, carpenter, sir,' said Hope.

He explained Mr Fitton's presence while the carpenter eased himself out of the berth. He was as thin as the gunner but much taller, with long solemn features and long greying hair parted in the middle and covering his ears. He was in shirt and breeches, and not until he had picked up his blue coat from a bench and put it on did he extend his hand to the newcomer.

'You are welcome aboard to be sure, Mr Fitton,' he said in a deep and musical voice.

Mr Fitton, who had spent some days ashore in Wales less than two years ago, didn't need telling that Mr Owen was a Welshman.

'You would be the more welcome, indeed,' the carpenter went on in the same measured tones, 'if you could testify that you are not accustomed to take the name of the Lord in vain.'

Mr Fitton blinked but recovered himself quickly. 'I believe I use a damn or two when strongly moved, Mr Owen,' he said gravely, 'but I don't put the "God" before it.'

Mr Owen wagged his grey head. 'I doubt the danger to your soul is the same,

Mr Fitton,' he said, frowning judicially. 'Howbeit, there was one among us—I name him not—with whom blasphemy was—'

'Now, now!' Hope cut in. 'He's ashore in hospital, Mr Owen. *De mortuis*—well, not exactly, but—'

'All men stand daily in the flame of God's judgement, Mr Hope!' The carpenter's voice rose dramatically. 'And if they're on beds of sickness they lie in it also. God is not mocked, and the recording angel sleepeth not. Whatsoever a man sayeth shall be—'

'That's right enough, Mr Owen,' said Hope hastily, 'and the captain'll have something to say if we don't show up on deck. After you, Mr Fitton—he's Methody,' he added as they climbed back up the ladder-way. 'It don't do to let him get started on salvation.'

Saville was still standing at the rail when they emerged on the after-deck. He turned a cold stare on them as they approached and touched their hats.

'Mr Sims died in hospital an hour ago,' he said abruptly; and without change of tone, 'Mr Hope, take two hands and get the cover off the longboat. Check all gear—plug, bailer, boat's bag, water-barrico. Mr Fitton, overhaul your cabin.'

'Aye aye, sir.'

'Wait. Mr Sims's valuables and best uniform went ashore with him but you'll find his seagoing coat and breeches in the cabin. Change those things of yours for them. He is—he was much of your size.'

'Aye aye, sir,' said Mr Fitton again, and went down the ladder-way.

Squeezing to the left at the bottom, he ducked into the cabin of the late Mr Sims. It was the merest hutch, half of its space occupied by a sleeping-berth two feet wide and six feet long with a cupboard above and a deep drawer under it. It had been recently swabbed-out, judging by the smell of soap. Hanging from hooks on the bulkhead that separated it from the captain's cabin were things that inevitably brought to mind the man whose place this had been, a place that would see him no more: a blue coat somewhat salt-stained, a sword, a tarpaulin overall, and a leathern flask suspended by its strap. In the drawer below the berth he found a pair of white breeches, well-worn but far more presentable than his own, and two pairs of white cotton stockings. There was also, to his great satisfaction, a pair of buckled shoes, which proved, on trial, to be only a trifle too large; his own shoes had borne him bravely over the rocky slopes of Malta and the hill-tracks of Sicily but now, despite his laborious cobbling, they would have disgraced a travelling tinker. The cupboard contained a sextant, a telescope, and a tattered copy of Norie's *Seamanship*.

Sitting down on his berth, which he was able to do by bending head and shoulders far forward to avoid the cupboard overhead, Mr Fitton reflected on his present situation. He was as destitute of possessions as a man could well be, having lost everything in the sinking of *Courier* and his subsequent misadventures. His much-thumbed copy of the *Enchiridion* of Epictetus had gone with the rest, and the comfort of refreshing his memory of the old Stoic's pungent philosophy was barred to him. *Learn to will that things should happen as they do* was his old stand-by and he could manage that pretty well by now. Especially, he told himself, as his Tutelary Genius, the Stoic's substitute for the seaman's guardian cherub, had brought him aboard *Snipe*.

Apart from his pleasure in her as a

thing of beauty he liked what he had seen of her crew. There was no doubt of their pride in their ship and that was something that never failed to make a happy ship's company. Her captain, he thought, was largely responsible for that pride; Saville's manner when he had said 'Mr Fitton will act as my first lieutenant' would have suited the captain of a crack frigate, and he had taught his crew to maintain their little vessel as if she was an admiral's flagship. His curt gruff-and-grim demeanour might be natural to him or it might be assumed as proper to a naval captain; or again (Mr Fitton speculated) it could be a mask concealing the scar of some past injury or fancied slight. Saville, like himself, had reached a post-captain's age without receiving promotion—perhaps that was what rankled. Whatever it was, it had resulted in a ship that was a model, outwardly at least, of what a small naval vessel should be. Her fighting efficiency, of course, was another matter, and so far as he had heard it had never been tested.

Mr Fitton became conscious that his reflections were being prolonged by his reluctance to put on a dead man's clothes. He got cautiously to his feet and began to

65

take off his coat, with some difficulty in the confined space which was to be his home for less than a week. The passage to Gibraltar, he told himself, would be a pleasure-cruise compared with his last voyage. There was little or no possibility of action on this one.

<h1 style="text-align:center">3</h1>

'*You* say,' persisted Mr Adey, jabbing a gnarled forefinger at the carpenter, '*you* say as how we rise again and go up to heaven—meaning me, James Adey. Is that so or isn't it?'

Mr Owen set down his mug of cocoa and ponderously shook his head. 'Not me, Mr Adey, the Holy Bible,' he said reproachfully.

'It don't prove it. It's firing a gun into a sea-mist when you don't know whether there's a Frenchman there or not. Now then. If I get to heaven—'

''Tain't likely,' put in the boatswain with a grin. 'You won't drop your hook there 'less you're saved, 'cording to Mr Owen. I s'pose you ain't saved, sir?' he added, turning to Mr Fitton.

'I think it very doubtful, Mr Knott.'

Mr Fitton ran a finger round inside of his damp collar as he spoke. It was very hot in the little cabin, where the four of them were taking refreshment—their last before *Snipe* sailed—at two bells of the last dog-watch. On deck it was now cooler, for the westering sun had abated its noonday heat and the crowded harbour with its tiers of houses rising above the quays basked in a golden glow instead of the brazen glare of a few hours earlier. Those intervening hours had increased Mr Fitton's familiarity with *Snipe* to the point where he began to feel that she was his ship.

The captain had had himself rowed ashore shortly before noon, presumably to attend to the affairs of his deceased lieutenant; apart from a curt order to have all ready for sailing on his return, and a stern reminder that no boat with a woman on board was to approach the cutter, he had said nothing to Mr Fitton, who was nominally in charge during his absence. The boat had returned without him just as the squeal of the boatswain's pipe heralded a rush of hands down to the mess-deck for dinner and a subsequent din of cheerful shouting and the beating of tin plates. Mr Fitton was surprised to find himself relieved to hear that din; the orderliness and quiet on board the cutter had seemed almost unnatural.

He took his meal in the gunroom, as the warrant officers' mess was called in *Snipe*. This being a Monday, it was cheese and duff, and the stuffy heat generated by five men sitting close together to eat hot food in a small cabin could not spoil the admirable flavour and texture of Joe Dung's duff. The argument as to the possibility and nature of an after-life had sprung up at this meal, and it was evidently a favourite and recurrent one. Mr Fitton had long experience of messes and messmates, and he knew that their conversation tended to revert again and again to the same topic with the same arguments, apparently to the added enjoyment of the arguers. Though wearying enough to a non-participant, this repetition seemed to have the effect of blunting the shafts of debate, and after the first day or two of a voyage no one ever lost his temper.

The dinner-time argument had been cut short well before one bell of the afternoon watch, the time of the rum issue. It was *Snipe*'s custom to make this issue on the mess-deck with the boatswain and one officer supervising, and as he stood beside Mr Knott and the two large barricoes Mr Fitton watched the long line of shuffling seamen, each with his pint mug, as they came up one by one to be served with their grog. Two parts water to one of rum was not Mr Fitton's idea of a palatable drink but every face wore an anticipatory grin; it was over fifty years since Admiral Vernon had ordered this dilution of the neat spirit and his sins had long ago been forgiven him. The faces would become familiar, with names attached, before they reached Gibraltar. Most were clean-shaven but one, a giant of a man, sported a blond beard; the boatswain, in bidding him hold his mug level, called him Woolley. And here came George Dancer of Gleadsmoss, with a shy half-smile at him, followed by the three pigtailed seamen, one of whom had an old scar running across forehead and eye and the bridge of his nose, and the eye itself fixed and glassy. There was not, he told himself as he regained the deck afterwards, a poor hand among them.

The rest of Mr Fitton's afternoon had not been idly spent. First he had made further inspection of the twelve carronades and listened to Mr Adey's reasons for his dislike of them.

'No acc'racy, not a shred of acc'racy,' was the gunner's verdict. 'More like mortars than guns, they are. All right, d'ye see, for vessels as is come board-and-board and is blazing away point-blank, but when's this barky going to do that, I ask you? No, sir. If we was a fighting-ship, which we ain't, our best chance is stand off and deliver acc'rate fire, and for that long sixes is the boys.'

'A long gun needs six hands to man it. With the carronade you can manage with a crew of three, even two at a pinch. And if you load with case-shot—you've case in store?—and give full elevation you can cut up an enemy's rigging very effectively.'

'Aye—at close quarters, and when you've said that you've said it all.'

'Not quite all, by your leave. A carronade can be loaded and fired twice as fast as a long gun. Surely that's something.'

'And it's something again that ten rounds can hot it up so it splits its barrel. Not that there'll be any splitting their barrels this trip, or any chance of it, worse luck—the gun-crews is as fast as practice drills can make 'em, but two-thirds of the men have never been in a sea-fight. O' course,' Mr Adey had added gloomily, 'we're supposed to run, not stand and fight.'

That was true. A cutter was built for speed and her main duty was to carry dispatches and mails; her guns gave her enough authority for such secondary duties as dealing with smuggling craft or intercepting blockade-running merchant ships, but her timbers were so light that a single well-aimed broadside from the guns of a frigate or even a sloop could sink her. Mr Fitton had put forward the arguments for carronades chiefly to hear Mr Adey talk, and now he conceded his own agreement.

'You're quite right, Mr Adey, and I'd go even further. It's the long-range gun that can find its target that will win the battles of the future, in my opinion. But we mount short-range carronades and we can't get rid of 'em so we'll have to make do.'

He raised a mental eyebrow at his own use of *we*. He had been on board less than a day, and that, in the first instance, as a passenger, and here he was talking like one of the ship's company.

'Aye—we make do,' returned the gunner

disconsolately. 'Gun-drill every forenoon on the way up from Gib, and the lads down to under two minutes, load to load. And where's the use? We'll be off Toulon in a few days' time but there's no French fleet there now and if there was a twelve-gun cutter couldn't do more than show her heels.'

'And she'd do that, right enough,' put in the boatswain, who had come up while they were talking. 'There ain't nothing afloat could overhaul this craft, given a fair wind and a middling sea. You was asking about the running bowsprit, sir,' he added to Mr Fitton. 'If you'll step for'ard I'll have a couple of hands take her inboard. Lyney! Goggin!'

Two men, both wiry and red-headed, sprang forward from the group at the starboard rail. At Mr Knott's brisk order they cast off lashings and grommets and hauled on the side-tackles, bringing the jibboom sliding back. It was done deftly and swiftly, and when the boom had been hauled out and made fast and the men dismissed Mr Fitton said as much.

'Drill,' Knott returned succinctly. 'Mr Saville, he's a rare 'un for drill—and rightly so, mind you. I'll not deny,' he added, 'as

Goggin and Lyney are as smart as any man on board.'

'They're Irish?'

'Aye—and never a quarrel between 'em, which is a wonder.' The boatswain paused and then went on in a lower tone. 'I'll tell you, sir, 'twixt you and me, the crew of this vessel's been a wonder to me since I jined at Portsmouth. I've served in five—no, six ships, all a deal bigger than this, and—well, you know what you'll get for a crew. Three out of every five a weakling or a skulker or a jailbird, as has to have the devil flogged out of him afore he'll pull his weight on a sheet. In *Snipe*, now, there's thirty-eight crew and all prime seamen—not a pressed man among 'em—all willing, all fond of their ship.'

'She's a ship to be proud of, Mr Knott. And the men seem contented to have no shore leave, which is another wonder.'

Mr Knott hesitated, glanced quickly round him, and lowered his voice still further.

'That's the captain,' he said. 'Mr Saville don't like women, and shore leave and women goes together, as you know. The men don't mind. They knows his trouble.'

'Trouble?'

'Crossed in love, sir, and cruel hard at that. Half of 'em's been the same way themselves, so they've got a sort of sympathy. They'll get their shore leave at Gib, where the women's a bit safer by reason of the regulations.'

Mr Fitton nodded. For nine decades Gibraltar had been a British possession and naval base, and the authorities had long ago established at least a partial control over its innumerable brothels. Mr Knott, perhaps feeling that he had been over-confident with a man who had only joined the ship that morning, changed the subject.

'There's but the one thing the men don't like about this ship,' he said, 'and that's her name. You was in *Curlew*, I think, afore you jined *Courier*? Well, you'd say from the name as *Snipe*'s the same class, but she ain't. Laid down in Chatham yard, she was, to a new design, and I'm told they're building two more, with names like *Cherub* and *Cheerful*. We reckon we ought to have been *Challenge*—but there was never any luck come of changing a ship's name, 'cept with a captured Frenchman. But she's different. Take the sheer of our bows—'

He plunged into a long and highly technical description of *Snipe*'s underwater lines, deck space, and rigging, to which Mr Fitton listened with interest until the boatswain terminated it by pulling an enormous watch from the pocket of his blue coat.

'We'd best get the boat away,' he said. 'The captain's to be taken off at eight bells and there's a half-hour to go, but it don't do to keep him waiting. We can take a sippet in the gunroom while that's doing.'

So it was while the boat was making the long pull to the Vittoria quay that Mr Knott's 'sippet' and the resumption of the after-life argument was taking place. Mr Fitton, giving his first order in his acting—and very temporary—rank, had posted Midshipman Hope at the after rail to give warning of the captain's approach, and Mr Owen was weightily and mellifluously explaining the importance of being saved when Hope's voice came down the ladder-way.

'*Snipe*'s boat, sir, two—hup!—cable-lengths off the port quarter.'

On deck the very air seemed to be coloured with the deep rose-hue of

75

approaching sunset that glowed on the houses rising above the harbour and the hills above. Catspaws wrinkled the reddened water and stirred the cutter at her moorings so that she strained gently like a living creature impatient to be rid of the leash; the *tramontana* was beginning to steal down from the fast-cooling earth of the uplands. Mr Fitton, standing beside the midshipman, saluted as the captain stepped on board.

'Boat inboard, and smartly!' Saville snapped as his foot touched the deck. 'Pipe all hands, Mr Knott.'

The instant shrilling of the boatswain's pipe was hardly necessary; the hands were on deck to a man, clustered expectantly amidships.

'We'll get under way at once, Mr Fitton,' growled Saville, darting a frowning glance at him.

'Aye aye, sir. Hands to unmoor ship and make sail!'

Mr Fitton ran to his station for'ard as he shouted. Behind him Saville's roar ordered Meyer to take the helm and a squat tow-headed figure passed him running aft. The hurrying men were still now, in three groups: one in the bows standing by cable and jib halliards, one with the boatswain at the main halliard amidships, and a third group right aft under Midshipman Hope.

'For'ard there! Cast off!'

Snipe was moored fore and aft with her bows pointing to seaward, and the light wind was over her stern. The bow cable was off the bitts and coming in fast with two seamen hauling and a third coiling down with speed and precision.

'Flying jib—hoist!'

There was no need to repeat Saville's order. The narrow triangular sail rose like a wavering flame in the sunset light, flapped and filled, was sheeted home. The cutter felt its pull, but before the after mooring could restrain her it was cast off and she began to draw through the water. An incoming tartane slipped past, her sails like giant rubies in the sunset light; someone shouted cheerfully and unintelligibly from her deck. Ahead on the bow the upper rind of the sun shot a last dazzling ray from the sea horizon and vanished, and farther to starboard the outer end of the breakwater stretched a thin black bar across a riot of smoky reds and yellows. The following breeze was strengthening.

'Mr Knott! Up mains'l!'

Over a thousand square feet of canvas soared smoothly skyward, topping-lift and mainsheet drew it into shape, and the long boom carried itself far out to starboard and was belayed. Outer and inner jib rose in turn and *Snipe* began to slip through the whispering water with her bowsprit pointing to the open sea.

'Mr Fitton!'

He trotted aft. 'Sir?'

'You'll take the middle watch,' Saville said briefly. 'I'll see you are called.'

'Aye aye, sir.'

'Before you go below, check the cable stowage.'

'Aye aye, sir,' Mr Fitton said again as the captain turned away.

He checked the cable stowage but did not at once go to his cabin, lingering by the rail to watch the fading colour on the hills behind fast-receding Naples. The breakwater was past now and the cutter, feeling the increasing breeze as she came out from the lee of the land, was sliding like a swan over the darkening waves. The faint singing of the wind in the shrouds, the hushed repetitive wash of water along the ship's side, made the music he liked best, and under his feet was the stir and thrill of as fine a little ship as heart could wish.

Mr Fitton had long ago learned the wisdom of dwelling in the present. Beyond Gibraltar was blank uncertainty; behind him were dark weeks of frustration. But in this moment he was fully alive again, and life was good. He threw a last look at the dying fires low in the western sky and went below to his berth.

3 *Snipe*'s Mission

1

Many thousands of four-hour watches alternating with four hours of sleep had gradually developed a kind of sixth sense in Mr Fitton. Some time-divining mechanism within his unconscious mind usually woke him a few minutes before he was due to be called for his watch-on-deck. He woke now to familiar sounds, the creak and groan of timbers and cordage and the hollow wash of the sea, but it was a second or two before he remembered where he was and how he came there. Simultaneously his senses gathered and resolved what he could feel and hear—the tilt of his berth, the cutter's recurrent roll, the broken rhythm of waves under her cutwater: *Snipe* had a fair wind and a moderate sea and was running with the wind over her starboard quarter. Her *starboard quarter*, so the wind must have changed; the northerly breeze on her course for Gibraltar would have been on her starboard bow, so it must have veered right round to south.

Feet clattered on the ladder-way and a bang on the cabin door was followed by a hoarse voice shouting that it was comin' up to eight bells, sir. He shouted an acknowledgement and slid cautiously out of his berth and balanced on the swaying deck of the cabin while he buttoned his breeches, no easy task since their late owner had been a considerably smaller man round the waist. So drastic a wind-change in so short a time, he was thinking, should have brought a marked change in the weather; perhaps it was on its way. He shrugged on Mr Sims's tight-fitting coat, took his hat, and climbed to the deck, where in the hazy starlight he narrowly missed collision with a dark figure hurrying aft to the belfry. He had noticed the little wooden belfry below the after rail, housing the small brass bell, with some amusement; cutters usually managed without one, and this was presumably part of Saville's attempt to make his little ship as like a crack frigate as possible.

The wheel with its spark of light from the binnacle was right aft, and Saville bulked large beside the smaller shape of the helmsman. The four double clangs of the bell sounded as Mr Fitton approached and touched his hat.

''Morning, Mr Fitton,' Saville said gruffly, leaving his junior, who hadn't expected so much courtesy, somewhat surprised.

'Here you have her,' he went on in the time-honoured ritual. 'All sail to the topmast squares'l, wind steady, course west-sou'-west a half west.'

'Course west-sou'-west a half west,' repeated Mr Fitton as in duty bound.

Surprise, though his tone showed nothing of it, made him speak slowly and distinctly, and he thought the captain hesitated for a moment before speaking again.

'I'm to be called if the wind changes,' he said abruptly, and went to the ladder-way.

At the coaming of the hatch he halted and stood for some seconds motionless, as if pondering. Then he stepped down to the ladder and disappeared below. Mr Fitton went to look at the binnacle. The lamplit dial beneath the brass hood showed the course Saville had named. He set that enigma aside for a moment.

'Who's this at the wheel?' he asked.

'Dowding, sir.' A youthful voice.

'Done many tricks at the wheel, Dowding?'

'This is me third, sir.'

'You've still a little to learn. Meet her gently as she starts her roll, then ease off again. That way she'll run just a trifle more sweetly.'

'Aye aye, sir.'

He went to stand at the weather-rail. Overhead the great concave mass of the mainsail rose to its peak against the cloud-filmed stars, its long boom lifting and dipping far out to port. The Pole Star hung mistily above the starboard quarter. The big chart of the western Mediterranean was before his mind's eyes and this course was taking them towards the southern tip of Sardinia. Well, there was no reason why a ship's captain should explain his actions to a subordinate, and no officer would be fool enough to expect it. Mr Fitton dismissed the matter from his mind and gave himself up to enjoyment of the present.

The wind, still quite warm, was light but steady, and sea was hardly ruffled by it. The cutter's motion was over the long slow swell, not through it as a frigate's or a 74s would have been, and her rhythmic

roll—all fore-and-aft-rigged vessels rolled
with the wind aft—added to the illusion
that she was flying across the surface; a
gull's motion rather than a ship's. The
rigging thrummed softly, the sails rustled
quietly, and he could hear the low hum
of talk from where the men of the duty
watch were squatting under the weather
rail, some up in the bows, a group near
the foot of the mast, and three aft, handy
to the cleats of the mainsheet. If this breeze
held there'd be no need to handle a sheet
during his watch. Craning his head far
back, he could make out the square-sail
on its topmast. He wondered a little about
that sail. Few captains would have hoisted
at nightfall a sail so tricky to take in, if
it became necessary, in darkness or a
sudden squall. Captain Saville, perhaps,
was in a hurry for some reason. The
thought had scarcely crossed his mind
when he became aware that the captain
had emerged from the ladder-way. Though
Snipe had no material quarterdeck there
was a theoretical one on this little after-
deck and Mr Fitton moved quickly across
to the lee side, the weather side being
customarily reserved for a captain.

'Mr Fitton!'

'Sir?'

'We'll walk, if you please.'

The *if you please* was unexpected and there was an indefinable change in Saville's harsh voice. Mr Fitton ranged himself alongside and they began to pace the deck, hands behind backs, turning together opposite the main hatch to walk back past the helmsman to the after rail, accommodating their steps to the list of the deck. They walked the eight paces between turns twice before Saville spoke again, with his usual abruptness.

'You're a Fitton of Gawsworth, I believe.'

It was a statement rather than a question, but as he seemed to expect an answer Mr Fitton, recovering from surprise, admitted that he was. They took two more turns in silence.

'They're aware of that for'ard,' Saville's growled words were just audible. 'One of the hands knows you, I collect. It's very well. Seamen are happy to obey orders from a man who is well-born. Even though, as in your case, he holds no commission.' He paused for another two turns. 'The Norfolk Savilles are a branch of the Mowbrays. There was a

86

Fitton and a Mowbray at the signing of Magna Carta.'

Mr Fitton having no comment to make, there was another long pause. When the captain spoke it was in a less confidential tone.

'You accepted my course without query.'

'Naturally, sir.'

'I'm taking the southern route to Gibraltar. My orders require me to touch at Minorca.'

This intimation that *Snipe* was to enter waters controlled by an enemy surprised Mr Fitton but he gave no sign of it.

'Yes, sir,' he said without expression.

Saville grunted; whether in approval of his incuriosity or in impatience it was impossible to say.

'There are other matters you should know of as my first lieutenant, Mr Fitton,' he said shortly. 'Come to my cabin at four bells of the forenoon watch.'

'Aye aye, sir.'

'And you, Dowding—steer small or I'll have you swabbing-down the heads.'

Without waiting for the seaman's 'aye aye, sir' Saville turned on his heel and went below, leaving Mr Fitton to consider what he had just heard.

Discovery of the master's mate's origins had clearly changed Saville's attitude towards him, and this he found amusing. Mr Fitton had never had any faith in the theory that noble blood automatically gave a man the right to rule over his fellows, or admitted him to membership of a select coterie, but this was obviously Saville's belief. He was right, of course, in saying that seamen preferred their commanding officers to be gentlemen of right, and a title was particularly dear to their romantic hearts. And the reverse was true; a captain who had started his naval career as one of themselves, who had 'come in at the hawse-hole', had a deal of lower-deck prejudice to overcome before he could achieve respect.

That knowledge of his descent should have reached the captain was no surprise. 'What's said in the wardroom at two bells they know on the mess-decks at four bells' was a naval saying that was just as true in the opposite sense, especially in a vessel as small as *Snipe*. Of course George Dancer had spread the story among his mates, and it had probably come aft by way of Leggett, the talkative little seaman who had brought their dinner to the gunroom and acted as captain's steward.

So the fact that he was a man of family—'one of us' would be Saville's mental phrase—meant that he could be admitted, though cautiously, to the captain's confidence. Mr Fitton's impression was that Saville, cultivating the Olympian aloofness of his courtesy rank to the extreme, would not otherwise have divulged anything of his purposes. It was impossible to imagine him revealing his orders and destination directly to his crew; he would do that as he had done just now, when he spoke of them loud enough for the helmsman to hear. And what of that remarkable destination? *To touch at Minorca*—Minorca, a Spanish island, enemy territory. That was odd. Mr Fitton, as he paced steadily to and fro beside the weather rail, reviewed what little he knew about Minorca. He had never sailed within sight of the Balearic islands, but he knew that they made a group of three, apart from the smaller islets, lying some 120 miles off the Catalan coast of Spain; he knew that the easternmost island, Minorca, had in Port Mahon one of the finest harbours in the Mediterranean, a harbour deemed impregnable from the sea. And that was all. One thing was certain: *Snipe*'s destination could not be Port Mahon. Beyond that speculation was useless and he was probably going to learn more tomorrow.

A rattle and a light flap from out on the boom caught his ear.

'Mainsheet, there!' he said sharply. 'Take in a quarter-fathom and belay.'

'Aye aye, sir.'

A change of wind on the way? There was more cloud across the stars than formerly. He resumed his pacing, letting his thoughts range on many things of past and present but always with eye and ear alert for that possible wind-change. It didn't come. The middle watch passed slowly, as it always did, and uneventfully except for the hourly coming of a seaman to sound the bells. The stars wheeled, peering fleetingly through light drifts of cloud; the cutter steadily left the dark sea-miles astern; and the four double strokes on the bell had scarcely sounded when Saville came up to take the morning watch.

Apart from the curt exchanges of the formal handing-over the captain had nothing to say. Mr Fitton, as he stripped off his coat and eased himself into

90

his berth, wondered whether he was regretting his lapse from the aloof and autocratic character he had set himself to play.

2

A thudding and shuffling overhead woke Mr Fitton halfway through his four hours of watch-below and told him that *Snipe* was scrubbing and swabbing decks; in this as in other ways adhering strictly to the naval routine observed in frigates and 74s. The hands mustered at dawn for this first rite of the ship's day. And when he came on deck to take the forenoon watch it was as if the world itself had received a scrubbing.

It was one of those mornings when merely to be alive and gifted with senses is sufficient. Cloudless blue sky and a sea only a little darker than the sky, the cutter's white sails dazzlingly luminous with sunlight, the spotless deck—all shone with the freshness of things new-made and unique; and Mr Fitton, who had seen hundreds of such mornings at sea, wondered again at his own exhilaration.

Even the touch of variant colour needed in all this blue and white was there: the bright red woollen cap affected by Mr Knott, who was up for'ard with half-a-dozen hands priddying the falls of the jib sheets. A fountain of spray, glittering silver, flew over the bows and drenched them as he looked, and the men screeched like delighted children.

The steep angle of the cabin deck as he dressed had told him what had happened and it was no surprise to find that the wind had backed three points and strengthened. It was now on the cutter's beam, and she was racing joyously across a ridged and white-capped sea with her tall mast canted far over and her lee rail almost leaning on the surface. She could be making ten knots, he told himself as he stepped across to where Saville stood beside the man at the wheel. The captain's spotless blue coat and white breeches made Mr Fitton uncomfortably conscious of his own ill-fitting clothes. The joyous morning found no reflection on Saville's face, which was grim and unsmiling as ever, and apart from the prescriptive handing-over of the deck he had nothing to say to Mr Fitton. He turned away, shouted for Mr Hope to give a cast of the log, and went down to his cabin.

The midshipman came trotting aft with the boatswain and a seaman in attendance. His salute and shrill 'Good morning, sir!' to the officer of the watch were succeeded at once by his orders.

'Up with the reel, Blower, and stand by. Ready—hup!—boatswain? Turn!'

On the word he tossed the wooden log overside and simultaneously Mr Knott turned the sandglass. The log-line streamed astern from the whirring reel held above his head by the seaman.

'Nip!' shouted the boatswain as the last grains of sand dropped, and instantly Hope's wiry fingers fastened on the log-line and he looked eagerly at the marks.

'Ten-and-a-half! By thunder, she's doing ten-and-a-half knots!' he yelled excitedly; and hastily recollected himself. 'Very well, Mr Knott. Reel in, Blower.'

He hurried below to report the speed to the captain. Mr Fitton checked the course, which was still west-sou'-west a half west, and bade the helmsman good morning. It was George Dancer at the wheel, and he would have liked to ask Dancer how he had come to join the Navy and when he had last seen his home in Cheshire, but conversation with a helmsman who had his whole attention fixed on course and ship was out of the question. Instead he set himself to enjoy the pure pleasure of sailing on a strong and fair wind; the steep heel of the deck, the rush of air and water, the thrust and bound of the cutter—a living creature, surely—under his feet. Saville, he saw, had sent a lookout to the masthead, but there was no speck on all the blue circle of water and *Snipe* seemed to have the whole Tyrrhenian Sea to herself. With a bowl of Joe Dung's excellent burgoo inside him (it merited more than the hasty five minutes he had been able to give it) and sun and sea lifting his spirits he asked nothing better.

For two hours *Snipe* held her course without a sheet being touched. A hand had just sounded four bells when Saville came on deck and raised his deep voice.

'Mr Hope! Mr Knott! Aft here. You'll be in charge of the deck for twenty minutes.'

He glanced at Mr Fitton, nodded curtly, and went below. Mr Fitton lost no time in handing over to Midshipman Hope and following the captain.

'Sit down,' Saville growled as he ducked into the cabin.

There was just room for the two of them to sit at the little table; the lockers, chart-racks and shelves of books considerably reduced the already confined space. A worn-looking chart was spread on the table, one end of it held down by a sizeable lump of rough granite to keep it from sliding on the tilted table. Saville's features (Mr Fitton thought) somewhat resembled those of the granite as he asked his first question.

'Have you ever sailed in the Balearic waters, Mr Fitton?'

'Never, sir.'

'Do you speak Spanish?'

Mr Fitton decided his few words of the language didn't amount to speaking it. 'No, sir.'

Saville received these two negatives unmoved, speaking straight on. 'You are aware of my situation. Midshipman Hope has little experience. Knott is a good man and reliable but with limited intelligence. If I were incapacitated, you, Mr Fitton, would of necessity take charge. I have decided, therefore, that you should know my orders.'

He paused, rather as if he had made a very surprising statement.

'Yes, sir,' said Mr Fitton.

'I am directed,' Saville went on in the same deep expressionless voice, 'to bring this vessel off a bay or cove called Cala Roqua on the coast of Minorca on the 14th of this month. There I am to take off a man named Doctor Miguel Oliviera at midnight, the word of recognition being "Gibraltar". Oliviera is a British Government agent—a spy, in fact—and yesterday a message from him reached the British envoy. He believes he is suspected.'

Mr Fitton, his interest now fully aroused, ventured an interruption.

'By your leave, sir. How did this message arrive?'

'I was told it was brought by a fishing-boat from Ciudadela, on Minorca. To continue. If the rendezvous fails I am to repeat it on the succeeding night and the one following. If those are unsuccessful I sail on the 17th for Gibraltar. The envoy adds to his orders two presumptions, how founded I do not know. First, that this Cala Roqua is to be found somewhere in the neighbourhood of Ciudadela, on the west coast of Minorca. Second, that Doctor

Oliviera's—uh—espionage is in preparation for a proposed invasion of Minorca by our forces. Now.' Saville, moving for the first time, bent forward with a forefinger on the chart. 'The course I intend to sail. My position by dead reckoning is here. The wind holding fair, I should raise Cape Carbonara by sunset. Sou'-west then west to clear Spartivento, then west-nor'-west for Minorca.'

Mr Fitton had been craning his neck to make out the minute details of the chart. It was an old chart, Caselli's, showing the western Mediterranean on a scale of something like fifty miles to the inch, and Minorca's thirty-mile length appeared as a very small oblong beside Majorca and Ibiza to the west of it. Mahon and Ciudadela were the only ports marked and the dotted fifty-fathom line the only soundings; a dot in the centre of the island was marked as 'Mt Toro 1770 ft.'

'Have you no other chart?' he asked, omitting the *sir* in his concern.

'No.'

'Then how—'

He checked himself; it was not for him to interrogate his senior. But how was the captain to be expected to find an insignificant cove on an unfamiliar coast without a proper chart showing soundings and a detailed coastline?

'I was told—' Saville growled out the words—'to accost a Minorcan fishing-boat and inquire my way to Cala Roqua.'

'It would have to be in daylight and probably within sight of an enemy shore.'

'Just so,' Saville paused. 'Have you any further comments, Mr Fitton?'

The question could have been sarcastic; but the tone was not. Glancing up, Mr Fitton found the captain's grey eyes fixed steadily upon him, and in them a strange gleam—a look, almost, of appeal—and he received sudden enlightenment. Behind that iron façade was a man who was in need of help though he would never ask for it, a naval officer confronted by problems too difficult for solution by himself alone. Saville would never have called this a conference, but that was what he wanted.

'I have, sir,' he said evenly, 'though no doubt you will have made them yourself. May I ask how long Oliviera has been on Minorca?'

'I was not told. I know only that he asks to be taken off earlier than was arranged.'

Mr Fitton, like Sir William Hamilton's secretary, had calculated times and distances. 'It will be nigh on a fortnight since his message was sent when we reach Cala Roqua,' he said. 'In that time he could have been taken, killed. Or he could have been tortured to reveal his plans, in which case the Spaniards might be waiting for us at Cala Roqua.'

Saville nodded, watching him. 'I'd thought of that. There's this too, Fitton. If they've any suspicion of an intended invasion—and God knows that's likely enough—they'll have vessels patrolling the coast. Their main fleet's in Cadiz by all accounts, but they're bound to have a frigate or two in Mahon. We can't fight a frigate. We'd have to run for it if we met one. We'd win clear, that's certain, but it would mean our presence on the coast was known.'

Mr Fitton hadn't failed to note the omission of the *Mr* and the substitution of *we* for *I,* and it pleased him.

'We'll have to chance it,' he said. 'If we can make a night approach to Cala Roqua—'

'Without a notion of where it is?' Saville cut in, frowning. 'That's the nub of the matter, Fitton—how to find the damned place. I tell you frankly I don't see my way.'

'There's a chance of catching a Minorcan fishing-craft—'

'There's altogether too much chance about this business. How the devil am I to search fifty or sixty miles of coastline unseen?'

'I fancy we may narrow it down, sir. A vessel secretly landing a spy on Minorca wouldn't approach Port Mahon, that being the Spaniards' chief naval base on the island. We rule out the east coast, then. The fishing-boat that brought Oliviera's message came from Ciudadela, a lesser port on the west coast, so it's probable that Oliviera's place of hiding—he must have one, of course—is not far from Ciudadela. Now.' Mr Fitton, warming to his work, laid a finger on the chart. 'Mahon being impregnable from the sea, a British invasion force would advance to take it from inland—from westward. They'd avoid Ciudadela and land on the west coast farther south.'

'You don't know that.'

'Of course not. But I'm guessing along the lines of probability. If I'm right, Oliviera will have been collecting information about that line of march and about the landward fortifications of Mahon. And his best base for that would be on the west coast south of Ciudadela.'

Saville, peering at the chart, gave a sceptical grunt. 'It's a possibility and no more, Fitton. I've still to find a man who'll tell me where Cala Roqua is, and if I find one he's got to tell me in English.'

'One of the hands may have some Spanish. With your leave, sir, I'll make it my business to find out.'

'Do so, if you please, Mr Fitton.'

The captain, once more aloof and formal, began to roll up the chart. Mr Fitton half rose from his chair.

'One other thing occurs to me, sir.'

'Well?'

'If Oliviera has succeeded in getting the information he was sent for—details of fortifications, numbers of garrison and so forth—it could well be of the utmost value to the commander of an invading force. It would be worth risking a good deal to—'

'I believe I know my duty, Mr Fitton!' Saville barked, glaring at him. 'Return to yours, if you please!'

'Aye aye, sir.'

Mr Fitton was halfway up the ladder-way to the deck when another bark arrested him.

'Mr Fitton!'

'Sir?'

'Thank you,' Saville growled.

3

'Cease fire!' roared Saville. 'Secure! Check all tackles, Mr Fitton,' he added over his shoulder as he went below.

'Aye aye, sir.'

There had been no firing; this had been gun-drill in the afternoon watch, with no powder and shot. It had been made possible by a lessening of the wind, which had not only reduced *Snipe*'s speed to eight knots but had also given her less heel, making it feasible for the 12–pounders to be run out on the starboard side. The men had rattled the carronades in and out rapidly enough, wielding their sponge-and-rammers with trained dexterity, but of the eighteen men only the three pigtailed seamen—Cheney, Witt, and Bolsover—had fired a gun in action.

Mr Fitton discovered this as he moved

from gun to gun among the crews, checking that every carronade was tightly bowsed-up and had its tompion in the muzzle. He used this opportunity to find out if any of the hands spoke Spanish, and found in George Dancer the man he was looking for.

'Aye, sir, I got a word or two o' the lingo,' Dancer said, with a reminiscent grin. 'Spent two months in a Spanish prison, I did, two year ago.'

'How was that?'

Dancer, it appeared, had only joined the Navy last year. Before that he had sailed in a trading brig which had been taken by a Spanish privateer off the Biscay coast, and his escape from the filth and maltreatment of a prison in Santander had left him eager for revenge.

'The lads are sayin' we'll get a chance at the Dagoes this v'yage, sir,' he said. 'Would that be right, now?'

Mr Fitton shook his head. 'Our job's to keep clear of them. Say this for me in Spanish—"where is Cala Roqua?"'

'*Donde esta Cala Roqua,*' Dancer replied promptly.

'You'd understand a reply in Spanish?'

'I reckon I could make a shot at it, sir.'

'Very well.' Mr Fitton raised his voice. 'Gun-crews dismiss! Duty-watch to stations!'

He was moving aft towards the helm, it being his watch-on-deck, when Mr Hope, who had been in charge of the three for'ard carronades, came up with him. The midshipman's youthful features were set in an expression of grim resolution.

'Sir,' he began; and stopped.

'Yes, Mr Hope?' Mr Fitton prompted after a pause.

Mr Hope gulped. 'It was—hup!—it was a good drill, sir. Leastways, I thought so.'

'It was well enough. You'll understand, though, that it's not easy to foresee how inexperienced men will behave in a real action. There are very different conditions when the shot is crashing and the smoke blowing—'

'That's just it!' Hope broke in with a kind of desperate eagerness. 'There's me—I don't know how I'll behave. I've never been under fire.' He mastered a hiccup. 'I ain't shy, far as I know, but I'm—well, I'm afraid, that's what it comes to. You've been in dozens of actions, sir, I dare say, and I wondered if—I wondered,' he finished lamely.

For a brief moment Mr Fitton's thoughts

flew back eighteen years to *Defiance*'s main-deck and the flame and thunder of that first terrifying broadside.

'You're afraid of being afraid, Mr Hope,' he said cheerfully. 'We all are, the first time. The remedy's simple. Forget yourself and remember your duty. What's your charge in an engagement?'

Hope looked surprised. 'Why, the for'ard guns.'

'Three carronades, nine men, and you're responsible for them all. You've to listen for orders, see the guns are properly pointed, keep an eye on powder and shot, be ready to deal with a hand killed or a gun dismounted—enough, surely, to fill any man's mind. Fill yours with it, Mr Hope, and keep it there.'

'I'll try, sir,' Hope said doubtfully. 'But—'

'Deck, there!' The hail from the masthead lookout silenced him. 'Two sail, sir, stabb'd bow.' Then, after a pause, 'Land-ho! Land-ho, sir!'

'Where away?'

'Stabb'd, sir, fine on the bow.'

Mr Fitton had Sims's telescope in his pocket. He hoisted himself into the weather shrouds and climbed the narrowing ratlines to the masthead. There was no top here as in a square-rigger and the lookout (it was Woolley) found standing-room on the cap at the foot of the squaresail topmast, to which he was secured with a rope round his waist; a precaution which the whip of the tall mast and its angle made necessary.

'Likely it's Sardinia yonder, sir?' said Woolley as he came up.

'It's very likely indeed.'

Mr Fitton hooked an arm round the topmast stay and focused his telescope. The two white specks on the horizon held his attention for a moment only; Sardinia, an appanage of Austria, had no part in the war and hostile craft off her coast were improbable. Beyond them his glass showed him the coast, a thin bar of pale brown lying along the blue rim of the sea, plain to see in the clear atmosphere of late afternoon. Far to the south the pale bar terminated abruptly in an obvious headland that must surely be Cape Carbonara at the south-east corner of Sardinia. Rounding that, he reflected, visualizing the chart, another seventy sea-miles would bring them off Cape Spartivento at the south-west corner and halfway on their passage to Minorca.

That should be early on the 12th, so there was a good chance of their reaching the rendezvous on the 14th, the first of the specified three nights; a better chance of that, he thought, than of finding anyone at the rendezvous.

Eight bells were sounded as he climbed down to the deck to find Saville waiting for him.

'Cape two points on the bow, sir,' he reported.

The captain bent to sight across the compass card. 'Sou'west half-a-point west,' he said curtly. 'Carbonara.'

'A good landfall, sir.'

Saville grunted. 'I'll take over, Mr Fitton.'

When he went below to the gunroom for his 'sippet' a few minutes later, Mr Fitton found the boatswain and the carpenter already there and engaged in argument. Somewhat to his surprise they were not, this time, arguing about the survival of the soul but about the weather.

'I tell you, Mr Knott,' the carpenter was saying, one hand raised like some biblical prophet, 'that these matters are ordained from Above. In the week before the equinox—'

'The week after,' corrected Mr Knott firmly.

'I say before. I tell you from my own experience, look you.' Mr Owen turned to the newcomer. 'Mr Fitton here will support me. I am saying, Mr Fitton, that the equinoctial weather, the variable winds, and the sudden storms, and other unusual portents—these, I say, come upon us a week before 21 September, which as we are told is the date of the equinox. You know this, to be sure.'

Mr Fitton shook his head slowly. 'To be honest with you, Mr Owen, I've not found the equinox makes much difference. The wind bloweth where it listeth, as usual.'

'And thou knowest not whence it cometh,' said Mr Owen, pointing an accusing forefinger at him. 'I tell you, sir, in '92 I was off Algiers in *Monmouth*, not a hundred leagues from where we sit—and, look you, at this very same time of year—when for three days we encountered storms, lightning and thunder, waterspouts, winds blowing round the compass, flames of fire on the ends of our yards. Oh, many, many, my friends, are the wonders of the Almighty!'

'Pity he don't keep that sort to himself,

then,' muttered Mr Knott.

The carpenter's sheep-like countenance stiffened into something approaching anger, but any retort he was about to make was forestalled by Lecky's arrival with three steaming mugs and a platter of bread.

'Last o' the fresh bread took on board at Naples, gennlemen,' said the steward. ''Tain't nigh stale yet, an' it's biscuit after this. I 'ear we're to touch shore at Minorca,' he added with a side-glance at Mr Fitton, 'but 'twon't be to take in bread, I'm thinkin'.'

Mr Fitton, cautiously sipping boiling-hot cocoa, made no reply, but he marvelled again at the speed with which news travelled in a small warship.

Mr Adey coming below to join them, Lecky was sent back to the galley for another mug.

'Wind's backing again,' the gunner said as he sat down. 'This weather won't hold long. I reckon we'll be into the dommed equinoctials in a week.'

'We are in them now, indeed, Mr Adey,' pronounced the carpenter in measured tones. 'I have been telling—'

'Not till after 21 September,' said the boatswain, setting his mug down with a thud. 'And for why? Because the days and nights being equal then begins to upset the air, see? What happened to you off the Barbary coast ain't evidence. I've seen a waterspout off that coast in March.'

'Waterspouts?' said the gunner. 'I can tell you of a waterspout—aye, and more than one. We was in the Genoa gulf, in the old *Belliqueux*—'

Mr Fitton listened to yarns and arguments until it was time to take over the deck for the last dog-watch.

The wind had backed, but only slightly, and *Snipe* held her course, a trifle more close-hauled, to bring Cape Carbonara abeam before sunset. It was a lurid sunset, with the sun sinking into long wreaths of smoky cloud, so that the ruffled sea glowed fitfully like the blown embers of a fire before purple darkness fell. Saville had steered to clear the headland by four or five miles, and at nightfall the south coast of Sardinia was still in sight with the course now west by south and the cutter close-hauled. Mr Fitton, having slept soundly through the first watch, came on deck for the middle watch and found Saville in what was for him a conversational mood.

'I've taken in the squares'l,' Saville said

gruffly when he had handed-over. 'No use close-hauled. This course will clear Spartivento. Coast distant four miles. You can see a light or two now and then.'

Mr Fitton took his opportunity. 'Some of the lights will be night-fishers, sir, boats close in to the shore. It's the usage on all the Mediterranean coasts and I don't doubt it's done on the Minorcan coasts too.'

'Well?' Saville growled as he paused.

'A suggestion, sir, for finding Cala Roqua. You make your landfall off Minorca's north-west corner—Ciudadela's three or four miles south of it—and disappear over the northern horizon. You close the coast at nightfall on a bearing to bring you south of Ciudadela, locate a night-fisherman by his light, and send a boat to question him. One of the hands, Dancer, has enough Spanish for the purpose.'

'And if there's no light, no fisherman?'

'Then our luck's out. But it's a better chance than stopping a fishing-vessel in the daytime.'

Saville was silent for some seconds. The faint light from the binnacle lamp showed his face grim and his lips pursed.

'Far as I can see.' he said at last, 'it's our only chance. And Oliviera's. I'll do as you suggest.'

He was gone into the windy darkness. Mr Fitton, beginning his pacing, reflected that this solitary chance depended on other things besides the absence or presence of a fisherman's light on a particular part of the Minorcan coast. There was wind and weather. High winds or high seas could make approach to the coast impossible. Oliviera's escape, perhaps the success or failure of the Minorcan invasion, hung on a very slender thread.

4 Uncertain Rendezvous

1

Mr Fitton was to remember those first two days of the Minorca voyage as the nearest thing to a pleasure-cruise he had experienced since joining the Navy. Two days of ideal sailing weather in a craft he had come to love, with a contented ship's company, no floggings, no threat of enemy interference—this was something rare indeed. The idyll of fair winds and clear skies seemed all the brighter, in retrospect, for its contrast with the two days that followed.

In the first grey light of 13 September they made their landfall off the dark headland of Cape Spartivento and took their departure from it, heading still westerly to clear the south-west coast of Sardinia. Morning came slowly under a raft of low hurrying cloud, and when the coast sank astern below the eastern horizon there was no sign other than a pallid lightening of the sky that the sun had risen. And the wind had backed still farther. At two bells of the morning watch, when Saville decided to bring the cutter on course for Minorca, it was blowing hard from the west-nor'-west, a head-wind for that course. He laid her on the starboard tack and summoned Mr Hope to record the legs of her zigzag course on the traverse board.

'Dead reckoning from now on,' he growled when Mr Fitton came up to take the forenoon watch. 'Shorten sail if you have to. Weather's worsening.'

Mr Fitton, left to himself, felt some surprise at being given this responsibility. Hitherto Saville himself had ordered changes of course or sails; now, apparently, he had decided that his temporary first lieutenant's seamanship could be trusted. With a man as careful of his ship as *Snipe*'s captain this was a considerable act of faith, and within an hour it was put to the test. Wind and sea rose with surprising rapidity, and it was plain enough that the cutter was over-canvassed. Mr Fitton had reefed sail in a cutter before now, but had had no dealings with running bowsprits and was a trifle relieved to see Mr Knott's red cap among the hands for'ard. He shouted his orders.

'Hands to reef mains'l! Mr Knott! Down flying jib and in with the jibboom.' Then, to the helmsman, 'Bring her to the wind, Goggin.'

Snipe's bowsprit swung and the long mains'l boom came amidships as the outermost of the three jibs sank flailing and snapping to be hauled inboard. The hands at topping-lift and main halyards lowered away and other men sprang to drag at the flapping canvas and tie-down the reef. Up went the yard again, the thunder of the loosened sail diminished and ceased, and, at Mr Fitton's order, Goggin, juggling dexterously with the wheel, brought the wind over the bow and she paid off with a sudden heel. A moment later she was back on her course, close-hauled and slicing through the tall green waves. It had been deftly and quickly done. However *Snipe*'s crew might show in a fight, there was no doubt of their capacity as seamen.

Mr Knott came trotting aft to report the running bowsprit inboard.

'Looks right dirty to wind'ard,' he added.

'We'll be wearing inner jib and full-reefed main afore noon.'

He was right. The afternoon watch found the cutter carrying her smallest canvas and battling with a veritable storm. The scudding clouds had come so low that her wildly-rocking mast seemed almost to scrape them as she plunged rising and falling across the seething white wilderness of sea. The waves were not the mountainous Atlantic rollers but they were steep and high, high enough to make a dark-green wall crested with white towering above *Snipe*'s bows until she rose to give a view of the wind-torn surface to the men on her deck. Except for its increased strength there had been no further change of the wind. Saville had taken his precautions: lifelines had been rigged fore and aft, the carronades double-lashed, Joe Dung's galley fire dowsed, two hands at the wheel. He sent Mr Fitton, who had not left the deck, down to the gunroom in the first dog-watch, telling him curtly to eat and drink what he could while he could.

Mr Adey and Mr Owen were there, nursing mugs of small ale which was the best Joe Dung could do for them with his fire out. The gunner had one hand on a platter of ship's biscuit to hold it in place on the swaying table.

'*You* say—' Mr Adey paused to nod at Mr Fitton as he sat down—'you say it's the equinoctials. *I* say it's the *gregale*. That's what they call it on Malta and it can blow any season.'

He lifted a pewter jug from beneath the table, where his foot had kept it from sliding, and skilfully filled a mug for Mr Fitton, who thanked him and helped himself plentifully to biscuit. Mr Owen wagged his head resignedly.

'Name it as you will, my friend,' he said, it is ordained from Above.' He rolled his eyes upward and intoned musically. 'By sea or land, we're in his hand. And look you, now. Not a sheet is handled in this vessel, not an order is given, but the Almighty ordains it. I say unto you—'

'You don't know it and you can't make so much as a guess at it—no man can't.' The gunner had been tapping the edge of his biscuit on the table as he spoke, and a diminutive weevil had duly emerged. 'See this little bugger. Think he could ever get as much as an inkling of what a ship is, or a man, or why he's going to die—'

he crushed the weevil with his thumb-nail '—like this? There ain't no way he could understand, and that's like us.'

Mr Owen, with a hand raised in apostolic protest, was evidently about to launch on an exposition of the merits of faith, and by way of those to the certainty of an after-life, but the gunner cut him short by turning to Mr Fitton with an abrupt change of subject.

'I hear it's to be west coast of Minorca, midnight tomorrow,' he said with a sharp glance. 'That right, sir?'

'Yes.' Mr Fitton knew better than to ask where he'd heard it.

'We'll make it, never fear. This is a *gregale,* as I've been telling old Equinoctials here, and if it don't blow itself out in another twenty-four hours I'm a Dutchman. Belay, there!'

Mr Owen, reaching for the last biscuit as Mr Fitton rose to return on deck, found it snatched from his fingers.

'By'r leave, sir.' Mr Adey dropped it into Mr Fitton's pocket. 'You'll find you'll need this.'

After the comparative peace of the little cabin the deck was a roaring tumult of wind and water. The roar of the seas and the shrieking of the wind made communication difficult even by shouting, and the sheets of spray that crashed continually on the deck to stream out through the lee scuppers added to the noise. On every side was a chaos of waves, tossing, leaping, hoisting threatening crests above the rail with a leer of white teeth as they rushed astern. In this madness of the elements *Snipe* seemed a lone embodiment of sanity. A creature of fixed purpose and indomitable will, she swept on her appointed way, shouldering aside the green walls of water and riding the foaming surges as though she revelled in her mastery. Mr Fitton lost his heart to her a second time, though he was well aware that that seeming mastery depended on her human masters. A moment's error at the straining wheel or in the handling of the sheets when she went about could mean the end of ship and crew in such a sea.

But Saville saw to it that there was no error. He was sticking stubbornly to his zigzag course, and at each putting-about his harsh voice cut through the din of the storm directing every detail of the operation. The spray-drenched hands at main and jib sheets obeyed his orders instantly. Only a skilled seaman could have coordinated helm and sails so that the hazardous moments when the cutter was paying-off on the new course were safely passed. His big tarpaulin-clad figure straddled on the tossing deck seemed a part of the ship.

The gale rose no higher but nightfall brought no abatement of its fury. All that night the cutter battled on through the roaring darkness, the watches changing at their due times, the helmsmen relieved every two hours, the three officers—Mr Hope huddled below the weather rail with his traverse-board—holding the deck. Dawn grew sullenly out of the east, revealing a heaving white waste below a low grey sky, and with it came the first slight lessening of the wind. *Snipe* rode the sea less furiously, and Saville sent Hope for'ard with orders for Joe Dung to relight the galley fire. Mr Fitton, standing beside him at the weather-rail, sensed a relaxing of strain in captain as well as vessel.

'It's moderating,' Saville said.

It was almost the first time he had spoken, apart from shouted orders, for eight hours. He had his lips close to Mr

Fitton's ears to make himself heard above the continuing tumult.

'She took it well,' he added. 'She's a good sea-boat.'

'I never shipped aboard a better,' Mr Fitton returned with sincerity.

'I'm—fond of her. Could almost say I'm wedded to her.' Saville was silent for a moment and then jerked a question.

'You married, Fitton?'

'No, sir.'

'Likely to be?'

'I have no plans in that direction.'

'Did you ever hear—' Saville hesitated —'the name of Caldecot, Lady Flora Caldecot?'

'No, sir.'

If Mr Fitton was anticipating some revelation of the captain's past he was disappointed. Saville's grunt sounded relieved and he said nothing for half a minute. When he spoke it was a deep growl scarcely to be heard above the wind.

'Ships and women—no comparison. You can rely on a ship.'

He went to look at the compass and turned with a resumption of his usual abrupt manner.

'Take the deck. I'm going below.'

And the storm continued to abate throughout the morning watch and into the forenoon; at two bells of that watch the wind was no more than a strong breeze, and instead of plunging through a threatening and turbulent sea the cutter was rising and falling over a succession of rollers crested only here and there with white. *Snipe*'s daily routine had been resumed. The lifelines were unrove, the deck swabbed, reefs shaken out of mains'l and jib; both watches had had their breakfasts. With two bowls of Joe Dung's burgoo inside him Mr Fitton, on deck for the afternoon watch, could look back cheerfully on a stressful nine hours wherein Mr Adey's fortunate ship's biscuit had been his only food. The gunner had taken the spray-covers off the 12–pounders and was busy with them, attended by a party of hands with rags and grease. Mr Owen, with more hands, was at work on the forehatch, whose coaming had been smashed by the one heavy sea that had broken over the cutter's bows; and the boatswain and two seamen were examining the gammoning of the bowsprit. A dense overcast still hurried across the sky and there had been no sun for the sight Saville had hoped to take at noon; but the horizon was dark and clear ahead and the overcast was slowly lifting.

Saville, who had been in his cabin for some time working with chart and traverse-board, came on deck and sent a lookout to the masthead.

'Dead-reckoning position puts us ten miles east of Minorca,' he said. 'More guesswork than science, but we'll have made little leeway, and if—'

'Land-ho!' from the lookout who had that moment reached the masthead. 'Broad on the port beam, sir.'

'By God, we've done it!' Saville started to climb the shrouds and paused to look down. 'We'll make that rendezvous yet, Fitton!'

For the first time since Mr Fitton had known him he was smiling.

2

There was little, as Mr Fitton told himself, to warrant the captain's elation, unless it was his own recent display of fine seamanship. He had brought the cutter to within a few hours' sailing of her objective but that objective had still to

123

be found. Short of a desperate landing to kidnap a Minorcan native and force him to show them Cala Roqua, the plan Saville had agreed to try was the only one they could devise; and that, dependent as it was on the weather and the presence of night-fishermen on the coast—not to mention several other imponderables—was not much less desperate than the other.

Mr Fitton would have denied that he was superstitious, and certainly he was less so than the majority of seafaring men. But he would have admitted to at least a half-belief in the proposition of his Stoic mentor Epictetus that he, like all men, had a Tutelary Genius watching his doings, and that this heavenly presence could approve or disapprove the course he chose to take. Had the *gregale* persisted instead of being so short-lived, he would have felt (though not with full conviction) that the course he was at present pursuing was ill-advised and would probably end in failure. As it was, with the sea moderating so rapidly and the sky giving no further hint of storm, he could tell himself that his Tutelary Genius gave a modified approval to continuance of a necessarily hazardous scheme.

That the game was worth the candle he was increasingly certain. In the present state of the war a fine naval base like Port Mahon would be of inestimable value to Britain and its taking a major victory. It had to be assumed that the British Government's spy had obtained the information he was sent to get; that being given, it was worth taking any risk (as he had told Saville) if there was still a chance of bringing it back. If the Spaniards had got hold of it—

'Fore and main sheets! Summers, steer nor'-west a half west.'

Saville had come down the shrouds, barking orders as he came.

'Mr Hope—Mr Knott! Take the deck. My cabin, Mr Fitton.'

The afternoon was darkening early below the heavy overcast and it was difficult to see details when they were bending together over the chart.

'North coast of Minorca. We're seven miles off. Three sail close inshore, small craft. A solitary tall hill—must be this Mt Toro—bearing due south.' Saville took ruler and pencil and drew a line. 'Here's our position, then—and thank God we've got one!'

'*Snipe* made better headway than your

dead-reckoning expected,' Mr Fitton commented.

'She always does better than expected,' Saville said without looking up from the chart. 'See here, Fitton. This is what I intend.'

Mr Fitton peered more closely. The north-west corner of Minorca island was about twenty miles south-west of *Snipe*'s new-found position. From that corner, which was a rounded cape, the coast ran south for ten miles, with Ciudadela's narrow inlet close to the cape and the coast of the larger island of Majorca twenty-five miles away to westward. The wide passage between the two islands, he reflected, would be the natural route to be taken by a Spanish vessel coming from Barcelona or Tarragona to Port Mahon—or for a French ship making contact with their allies on Minorca.

'If we're to make this rendezvous at midnight,' Saville was saying, 'we've seven hours to do it in. We're heading west-nor'-west now but I shall alter course to close this headland at the tip of Majorca island—damned if I can make out its name.'

'Cape Formentor, sir, it looks like.'

'Yes. Well, Formentor's twenty-two miles from us so I can get a landfall there before it's too dark to see. Then west, two hours' sailing, to the coast south of Ciudadela.'

'You rely on the wind holding fair.'

'I have to rely on every chance holding fair. Including your night-fisherman, Fitton.'

'Not mine, sir. You could rely on him if he was.'

Saville was not amused by this mild attempt at humour.

'I'll remind you, Mr Fitton,' he said stiffly, 'that I'm endangering my ship by closing an enemy coast of which I have no chart or knowledge.'

'I beg your pardon, sir.'

'Very well. If we see your—if we see lights indicating night-fishermen working inshore, we send a boat to question them. You will go in the boat, with Dancer and two seamen. If you wish to comment pray do so.'

Mr Fitton concealed a smile. 'No comment, sir, but a suggestion. These Minorcans must trade with France, their ally, and the men may have some French. It would disarm suspicion if I said that we were from a French ship.'

'You speak French?' Saville demanded.

'Enough for the purpose.'

'That's well thought of, Mr Fitton. For the purpose, *Snipe* shall be a French sloop. Of what name?'

'I suggest *La Bécasseine,* sir.'

'Why?'

'It's ill luck to change a ship's name and that's the French for "snipe".'

'It will serve.' Saville's gravity was unmoved. 'What time is moonrise?'

'Two bells of the first watch, sir. It's half-moon, and with this overcast—'

'I'm aware of that. The darker the night the better.' He glanced again at the chart, peered at the Harrison chronometer on the bulkhead, and rose to his feet. 'On deck, if you please.'

It was near the end of the first dog-watch and a premature twilight hung over sea and sky. The smooth rollers over which *Snipe* steadily rose and fell showed no glint of white under the low grey sky, and the wind, which was rapidly moderating, had backed still farther. When Saville's orders brought the cutter on her course for Cape Formentor she was able, close-hauled, to hold it. With the change of the watch the masthead lookout was relieved and the new man warned of the landfall to be expected ahead. Twice during the next hour a sail was reported, both hull-down on the northern horizon and both passing from sight after a few minutes. Mr Fitton reflected that even if *Snipe* were to be sighted by a Spanish warship she was unlikely to arouse any suspicion of her identity; the cutter rig (the squaresail had not been hoisted) was not common in the Mediterranean but from four or five miles away she could be taken for a fishing-boat.

He had been amidships with Mr Knott making sure that the cockboat was ready for launching. *Snipe* carried two boats, and the much larger longboat was secured on deck abaft the mast, with the cockboat, a carvel-built eleven-footer, lashed above it. Saville's choice of the smaller boat for the inshore venture was a wise one. The sudden advent in darkness of a longboat manned by a dozen seamen might well lead any fishermen there might be to dowse their lamps and scuttle into cover.

''Less the captain orders otherwise,' said Mr Knott, 'Blower and Witt's your best men for the oars. Dancer, he can take his ease like a gent in the bows. 'Tain't likely you'll land, as I unnerstand?'

He seemed to know all about the coming operation though Saville, as usual, had said nothing about it to his crew.

'I've no intention of landing,' Mr Fitton said.

'Arms to be taken, sir? There's cutlasses and pistols in the gunner's quarters but he'll need captain's order to issue powder and shot.'

'No arms. I'll thank you, Mr Knott, to warn Dancer and Blower and Witt to stand by, though it'll be two or three hours before they're—'

'Sheets, main and fore!' Saville's roar cut him short. 'Ease away—belay!'

Snipe began to sail more smoothly as her mainsail-boom widened its angle. The boatswain sniffed the air and wagged his head.

'Backing wind's never a good thing,' he said. 'If it shifts to the south look out for squalls.'

'Equinoctials?' suggested Mr Fitton.

Mr Knott grinned. 'Calling names won't alter 'em. Anyways, 'twon't be too big a sea for the cockboat come another two hours.'

Saville's bull-roar summoned Mr Fitton

to take the deck for five minutes and he went aft to the helm. Already darkness was falling and the binnacle lamp had been lit, and he wondered whether there would be enough light left for the Majorcan landfall. He was standing at the after rail watching the grey trail of the cutter's wake widening astern when a massive hiccup apprised him of Mr Hope's presence behind him.

'Your pardon, sir,' the midshipman said as he turned. 'It never gives me any warning.'

'Have you tried to get rid of it?'

'Tried everything. Brandy, holding my breath, dill-water, stewed daisies—that was the wise-woman at Milton—and none of 'em worked. My examination for lieutenant comes up next time we're in a home port—that's before three captains as you know, sir—hup!—and I can just see their faces if I keep interrupting my answers with a—'

'Land ho!' came the lookout's hail from the masthead.

'Where away?' shouted Mr Fitton.

'Right ahead, sir—dead ahead.'

Saville had come on deck and was peering at the binnacle. He straightened himself to hail the lookout.

'What do you make of the coast?'

The reply came after a moment. 'Too dark to see much, sir. Could be an island, or a point, like.'

'Very well. Come down on deck, Cheney. Stand by to go about!'

His orders brought *Snipe* round through the wind to steady on the starboard tack, her new course south-east by east. With the falling wind now just abaft the beam she headed for the coast of Minorca, twenty miles away in the thickening darkness.

3

No seaman ever likes sailing to a time-limit and the more he thought about *Snipe*'s present programme the less Mr Fitton liked it. When she turned to head for the Minorcan coast it had been precisely at the start of the first watch, and her deadline for arrival at Cala Roqua was the end of it—midnight; she had four hours in which to complete the most difficult part of her mission. In that time she had to close an unfamiliar coast in darkness, find some means of locating the place of rendezvous, and (if that uncertain source of information was found) get to Cala Roqua and land there. It was true that if tonight's rendezvous failed the two succeeding nights—according to Oliviera's message—could be used, but to linger off an enemy coast through another day meant grave additional risk. There was a hit-or-miss quality about the whole business that irked his tidy mind; and as he stood on the swaying after-deck, with Saville's big black figure, outlined against the faint glow from the binnacle lamp a few paces away, he sought to reassure himself by looking at the things in their favour.

The sea was only slight now, which meant that night-fishermen—if there were any—would find it possible to ply their trade. The wind seemed to have steadied in the south-west, a fair quarter for their course, and it was a stiff breeze giving the cutter a good seven knots; before three hours had passed, then, the cockboat should be away on her uncertain mission. And the night, dark though it was, was not totally black. The raft of cloud overhead was evidently thinning, for by now—halfway on their course—the demarcation between black sea and dark-grey sky was plain, and behind the clouds over the port bow a faint radiance showed where the half-moon had risen.

Saville, who had not spoken for some time, turned from his stance abaft the helmsman.

'This course should bring us off the coast two miles south of Ciudadela,' he growled. 'God knows what that coast's got in the way of outlying rocks.'

'The chart marked a rock or islet a mile or so out from the southern point,' Mr Fitton recalled.

'There could be a score of others. I'll sound my way in, but I'm damned if I'll take her closer in than a half-mile. And that's only if I see any lights at the water's edge.'

'Speaking of lights, sir, we may see lights in Ciudadela. They'd give us a position by bearing and distance.'

Saville grunted and returned to stand at the shoulder of the man at the wheel. His anxiety was obvious and Mr Fitton could sympathize with it. *Snipe*'s timbers were not stout enough to withstand the impact of a reef, and should she strand on such an impact there was no tide to lift her off; she would be seen with the coming of daylight and the end of it for officers and crew would be a Minorcan jail.

The veiled radiance of the climbing moon gave a clear silhouette of the Minorcan coast when its narrow irregular bar lifted above the black line of the horizon ahead. It was evidently not a coast of high cliffs, for less than half an hour after sighting it they were near enough to see two tiny sparks of light well above sea-level; three more pricked into view a few minutes later. This must be Ciudadela, thought Mr Fitton, and wondered whether the fort up there (there was bound to be one) kept a lookout by night. Saville bent over the compass and took a quick bearing.

'East by north and three miles off. Port your helm, Dowding. Steady as she goes. Mr Hope, get for'ard and start the lead. Mr Knott! Take in the two outer jibs. Hands to reef mains'l!'

His orders set the cutter heading straight in for the coast, more slowly now but still making four or five knots with the wind on her starboard quarter. From forard, where the leadsman swung his 25–fathom line, came the regular splash and chant.

'No bottom with this line...no bottom with this line...'

135

For ten minutes the monotonous litany repeated itself while *Snipe* crept in towards the rising black rim of the land. The change brought a new note to the leadsman's voice.

'Bottom, sir!... By the mark twenty... deep eighteen...deep eighteen...by the mark seventeen...deep sixteen...'

The lights of Ciudadela had vanished, hidden by some undulation of the coast, and ahead were three planes of varying darkness: the faintly luminous grey of the sky, the jet-black outline of the land rugged-crested against it, and the dark glimmer of the sea at the foot of its cliffs. Those cliffs, thought Mr Fitton, could hardly be as much as fifty feet high; it was, indeed, impossible to tell whether they were cliffs at all or merely the slope of the land. His gaze, like that of Saville and Hope and a dozen others, was fixed on the sea at the foot of the cliffs. There was no glimmer of lanterns to be discerned there.

'...deep twelve...by the mark ten...'

Saville smote both hands on the rail and swung round. 'Hands to the sheets! Helm a-starboard!'

He kept his voice down; they were little

more than half a mile off now. He brought the cutter nearer to the wind, shaping a southward course parallel to the shore. His further orders placed a lookout in the bows and an anchor-party standing by. Mr Knott already had the cockboat's crew and the launching-party ready at the rail. But all, it seemed, was in vain. The dark shore passed slowly astern, its features indecipherable; the leadsman's continuing chant gave never less than eight or more than twelve fathoms below the cutter's keel; and no spark of light showed itself anywhere.

Mr Fitton, his eyes sore with staring into the dark, felt a moment of despair. His idea of seeking night-fishermen had been tenuous enough in all conscience but he had allowed himself to place faith in it, and now it had failed. This west coast of Minorca was only ten miles from north to south and they were more than halfway down it; the likeliest place for night-fishermen was near the only port marked on their chart, Ciudadela, and that was six miles astern now. He was considering the desperate alternative of pulling along the coast and visiting every likely cove (though they could hardly find it by midnight) when a curious squawk, an excited exclamation mingled with a hiccup, came from Midshipman Hope.

'Thought I saw a glimmer, sir,' he added. 'Yes—coming on the beam, sir! Two, three—'

'I see them,' snapped Saville. 'Bring her to the wind, Dowding. Mr Knott! Let go anchor. Halyards! Down main and jib.'

Some invisible headland or rock-reef had slid aside as they passed, revealing a row of irregularly spaced lights low down on the water. There were seven of them, close inshore.

'Felicitations, Mr Fitton,' Saville growled. 'There's your men. See what you can do with them.'

'Aye aye, sir.'

Mr Fitton dived down the ladder-way to his cabin and took Mr Sims's sword from its hook on the bulkhead. He doubted whether Minorcan peasants would show hostility to a strange boat, but for a delaying hand grasping a boat's gunwale a sword might be very useful, and he had therefore amended his decision not to go armed. When he regained the deck the cutter was swinging slowly round to her anchor and the hands were gathering-in the lowered sails. He ran for'ard, buckling on the sword as he went, and found the cockboat already in the water with her oarsmen in her and Dancer just climbing over the rail. He lowered himself into the sternsheets and gave the order to push off.

'Good luck, sir,' said the boatswain's voice from astern, and *Snipe* shrank away into the night.

As the cockboat rose and fell over the long smooth swell he could see the little orange lights ahead, less than four cable-lengths away. They were moving, closing together. At that distance and with the wind blowing onshore they must have heard the noises of *Snipe*'s anchoring, though the light from their fishing-lanterns would prevent them from seeing her. Would the men pull ashore and land? A deep nick in the skyline above the bay or cove where they were fishing seemed to suggest a way down to the shore there, with perhaps a village beyond the crest.

'Stretch out,' he told the two oarsmen. 'And attend to me, now. This is a boat from a French ship and I shall hail the boats yonder in French. Blower and Witt, you'll keep your mouths shut. Dancer, you'll speak only when I tell you to.'

'Aye aye, sir.'

The orange lights were bunched close together now. No doubt they were discussing the unusual phenomenon of a vessel anchoring off that unlikely part of the coast. Mr Fitton, one arm on the tiller, turned to look astern and found that he could just make out the anchored cutter. The moon was shedding a diffused light through the clouds, sufficient to show him the rugged features of the oarsmen and Dancer's protruding ears: sufficient, too, to reveal that they were entering a bay perhaps a quarter-mile wide and half that distance deep, between low reefs of rock. Across the water to starboard the embracing reef lifted its middle section in a sharp black pinnacle.

The lights—he could see boats and the figures of men now—were 200 yards ahead. Unexpectedly, the lanterns and the glint of water woke half-forgotten memories and for an instant he was a boy again, night-fishing in the reedy Wheelock with a home-made trident and an old dark-lantern. Then he was back in the present with its need for action. He raised his voice in a loud and confident hail.

'*Ohé, là! Ici le bateau de Bécasseine, chaloupe de guerre. Comment ça va, mes amis?*'

That might establish his identity or it might not. There was a murmur of gruff voices and then a single voice shouted 'No entiendo!' At least they, or one of them, spoke Spanish, then; he had half expected to find that they had only their own Minorcan tongue.

'Way enough,' he said, low-voiced. 'Dancer, when I bring her round bid them good evening in Spanish and ask where is Cala Roqua.'

'Aye aye, sir,' muttered Dancer.

The boat glided on, losing way, and when the lantern-hung fishing-boats were a short stone's-throw away Mr Fitton put his tiller over and she lay rising and falling on the gentle swell.

'*Buenas tardes! Donde esta Cala Roqua?*'

Dancer's question brought an instant response, a dozen voices speaking all together. Several of the shadowy figures in the boats were jerking their arms out sideways, pointing down the coast to southward.

'Ask how far,' Mr Fitton said quickly.

Again Dancer questioned, and this time

there was a unanimous shout of what sounded like *'Cerca, cerca!'*, followed by a deep voice delivering a brief lecture of which Mr Fitton could make out only two words—*arena* and *iglesia*. Dancer chimed in, seemingly repeating what he was told. Then he spoke over his shoulder in an undertone.

'Got it, sir!'

'You're sure?'

'Sartin sure, sir. 'Tis—'

'Thank them and say goodbye. Give way, men.'

The oars dipped and Mr Fitton headed the cockboat for the open sea, while Dancer shouted farewells: *'Convenido! Muchas gracias! Adios!'* A chorus of shouts, questions by the sound of them, receded astern.

'Now, Dancer.'

'Yes, sir. Struck lucky, we has. Cala Roqua's next bay south'd o' this un. Small, they said, with a beach o' white sand.' Dancer chuckled. 'Had me flummoxed when they said 'twas t'other side the church, but iglesia—that's church—is what they calls that big spike o' rock over there to port.'

'You've done well,' Mr Fitton said.

His level tone concealed his elation. The

142

long shot had come off after all and it had come close to being a bull's-eye. Now for the rendezvous—and here was a problem, for he had no accurate idea of the time. It must, he thought, be less than three-quarters of an hour to midnight; which gave little enough time—unless he took the cockboat straight round into Cala Roqua. No. That wouldn't do. He would be acting without orders and his duty was to report to Saville as quickly as possible. Saville might decide to go ashore himself, or to send the longboat, and he had the sole right of making decisions. A half-mile pull out and the same inshore again—there was still time.

'Quicken stroke, Blower,' he said, 'and stretch out, the pair of you.'

The cockboat pulled out from the little bay and the low headlands on either hand fell astern. From so low on the water it was not at first possible to make out *Snipe*'s single bare mast in the darkness and he told Dancer, in the bows, to stand up and see if he could sight her.

'Yonder she is,' the seaman said after a moment. 'Fine o' the port bow, sir. And—*hellfire!*' His voice rose suddenly. 'Sail, sir—port beam!'

Mr Fitton twisted round on the thwart. There on the screen of night shapes of a paler darkness moved slowly—the sails of a ship.

5   The Xebec

1

'Pull!'

Mr Fitton's urgent command was scarcely necessary. The men at the oars knew as well as he did that any ship in these waters, merchantman or ship of war, was an enemy. Blower, a squat seaman of great muscular strength, strove mightily at the stroke oar with Witt doing his best to match him and the cockboat leaped across the black waves like a flying fish. A cable-length ahead *Snipe*'s mast drew a thin perpendicular line on the night sky, and Mr Fitton could spare a glance or two for the strange sail.

She was barely a mile away and coming up fast, her hull all but invisible but her rig discernible in the dim light from the clouds. Not a big ship, but ship-rigged, carrying main and topsail on her foremast. She altered course as he looked, heading

145

straight for *Snipe,* and now he could see
her other two masts, square sails on the
main and a lateen sail on the mizen. A
xebec, then. He had heard that the Spanish
were building a class of small frigate with
the xebec rig. And no merchant ship
making a night passage would come so
close inshore, so this was a warship, out
of Port Mahon and patrolling the coasts.
Had Saville seen her?

That question was quickly answered.
The cockboat was only a pistol-shot away,
and the steady clank of the pawls of the
little capstan on *Snipe*'s foredeck sounded
clearly: the cutter was drawing up to her
anchor. Another ten seconds and he was
putting the tiller over to sheer alongside.

'Boat your oars!' He stood up. 'Boat
inboard and sharp about it!'

On the last word he hauled himself up
over the rail. Saville came striding to meet
him; beyond his big dark figure the ghostly
sails of the xebec loomed, closing fast.

'We've to run for it,' Saville said rapidly.
'I need two minutes more, Fitton. Hold
them with a parley if you can.'

'Aye aye, sir.'

He ran for'ard as he spoke. Hands
were clustered ready at the halyards,

others toiled at the capstan bars. Mr Fitton, dodging between Mr Hope and the boatswain, sprang on to the butt of the bowsprit, steadying himself with a hand on the forestay. The xebec had drawn almost level and was turning into the wind with her backed topsail flapping; a single-decker, twice the length of *Snipe*. He could just make out the ten gunports in her side and they were not open. She was barely within hailing-distance on the cutter's seaward side but he shouted at once, at the full pitch of a powerful voice and with as much bullying arrogance as he could command. And he shouted in French.

'Ahoy! What vessel's that and what are you doing here?'

There was a pause, probably of surprise and doubt, before the answer came, in slow and careful French.

'His Most Sacred Majesty's ship of war *Santa Brigida*, monsieur. Who are you?'

Behind him the capstan pawls clanked on. He delayed as long as he dared before replying.

'The Republic's ship of war *Bécasseine*. Stay hove-to. I shall send a boat.'

There was another pause and into it

spoke Mr Knott's voice.

'Cable's up and down, sir.'

Saville's bark followed instantly. 'Hoist away! Main halyard and haul for your lives! Up outer and inner jibs!'

The xebec had found her voice again and the words came distantly but with a new decision. 'We shall send our boat to examine you. It is our duty—'

The shout ended in a screech. *Snipe*'s sails were up and filling. Slowly she paid off on the port tack, heeled, righted, and gathered way, while her anchor swung dripping up to the cathead. A confused yelling from the xebec came to Mr Fitton's ears as he jumped down from his perch and ran aft.

It had been neatly and swiftly done but someone aboard *Santa Brigida* had not been slow to counter the move. With her foretopsail once more drawing the xebec was moving forward across the cutter's course; close-hauled as she was, *Snipe* was heading for a direct collision. Her way of escape was plain—to turn to starboard, away from the wind, and head towards the coast. But Saville was not going to risk his beloved command any nearer an unknown shore—a lee shore at that.

Shouldering the helmsman aside without ceremony and bawling *'Sheets!'*, he grasped the spokes and put the wheel hard over to port. The long boom hissed across and the cutter spun round like a top, heeling steeply and then righting herself close-hauled on the opposite tack. The movements of both vessels had considerably lessened the distance between them, and *Snipe*—now making five or six knots—was within a few fathoms of the xebec's lofty stern. Mr Fitton found he was holding his breath. The tall lateen sail seemed to pass directly above his head as *Snipe* flew past a biscuit-toss from *Santa Brigida*'s rudder-post.

'By thunder!' muttered Hope, at Mr Fitton's elbow. 'The Dons could've spat on us!'

'I trust they have better manners, Mr Hope.'

As he spoke, it occurred to Mr Fitton that he had yet to report the result of his mission in the cockboat—he had not once thought about Cala Roqua since the xebec had been sighted. He glanced at the captain, a few paces away beside the wheel. Saville had handed over to the helmsman again—and was standing tense and alert with his attention fixed on course and sails.

149

This was not the moment to report even a successful mission; if 'successful' was the right word. For though Cala Roqua had been located, the rendezvous at midnight there could not now be kept. He turned to look astern. Saville's daring manoeuvre had caught *Santa Brigida* on the wrong foot but she was not slow to correct her mistake. Already she was turning through the wind and her topgallants were filling on the yards. Beyond her shadowy sails the black uneven rim of the coast was beginning to dwindle and sink. She steadied close-hauled on the pale widening path of *Snipe*'s wake. It was to be a stern-chase, then, for Saville had no need to manoeuvre; the cutter, as close to the wind as he could steer without pinching her, had only to hold her present course and she must eventually leave the xebec far astern. Mr Fitton had seen enough of *Snipe*'s behaviour under sail to be sure that she could outsail the Spaniard. At this initial stage of the race, however, *Santa Brigida* was little more than a cable-length astern of her quarry.

Saville spoke suddenly. 'Your report, Mr Fitton, if you please.'

'Yes, sir. I entered a small bay and

questioned the night-fishermen. I learned that Cala Roqua is the next cove to south'rd of that one, identified by a conspicuous rock-pinnacle and a beach of white sand. We could have reached it—'

He checked himself. A bright red flash blazed briefly from the xebec's bows and was followed a moment later by the heavy report. There was no sign of the shot. In addition to her twenty guns, then, *Santa Brigida* mounted a forechaser. Since there was nothing to be said about it both Saville and his temporary lieutenant made no comment and Midshipman Hope's statement of the obvious sounded in a silence.

'She—hup!—she missed us.'

It was the first time he had been under fire, Mr Fitton remembered. 'She'd be lucky to hit us in this light,' he muttered reassuringly.

He was trying to gauge the passing minutes. He had estimated four when the second flash and bang came, again with no sound or sight of the shot. That suggested that the Spanish gunners were not well accustomed to their weapon.

'Sir!' The gunner had come aft. 'That's an 18–pounder long gun, sir.'

'I'm aware of it, Mr Adey.'

There was a pause before Mr Adey spoke again, hesitantly.

'Sir!'

'Well?'

'By'r leave, sir—load and run out?'

'No.'

'Aye aye, sir,' said the gunner resignedly, and departed for'ard.

It was a case, Mr Fitton decided, of enthusiasm outrunning common sense. Mr Adey knew perfectly well that *Snipe*'s 12–pounders stood no chance against a vessel of twice her size, nearly twice her force, and probably twice her number of crew. Nevertheless, he was conscious of an irrational sympathy with the gunner; it was galling to run away.

The forechaser fired again, and this time the Spanish gunners were nearer their mark. There was a crescendo humming, loudening to an eldritch shriek as the ball passed, overhead and to starboard. He caught a word or two from Mr Hope, who seemed unaware that he was speaking aloud.

'I didn't duck, I didn't duck,' said Mr Hope with satisfaction.

From the position of that third flash, as

Mr Fitton observed it, it was evident that *Santa Brigida* was losing the race, for it came from farther to leeward than the others. Unable to sail as close to the wind as *Snipe*, the xebec was sagging away from the course; and she was falling astern, too. Another ten minutes and they would be beyond the range of that long eighteen. The reminder that they were still within range was a sharp one.

He was watching to mark the fall of shot when the xebec fired her fourth, and saw the small white drift of spray from a wave-top. Half a second later he almost lost his balance as *Snipe* lurched and shuddered and a shower of splinters flew past the rail. The ball, falling short, had ricochetted to strike a grazing blow along the cutter's side on her port quarter.

A howl of execration came from the hands and one huge voice rose above the rest: 'Keep yer bloody paws off our paintwork!'

'Silence for'ard!' roared Saville. 'Mr Owen!'

But the carpenter had already come running aft, with Mr Knott at his heels. He draped himself head-downwards over the rail with the boatswain hanging on to his thighs and groped in the darkness along the cutter's side, muttering angrily as he did so.

'The sons of Belial!' he puffed, regaining a safe position. 'A groove in the top strake, sir, two fingers deep—'

'Is the planking sprung?'

'Not that I can feel, sir. The Lord protects his own—'

'Very well, Mr Owen. Mr Knott, slack off the outer jib-sheet a trifle, if you please.'

The two warrant-officers departed for-'ard, where the hands were still grumbling resentfully among themselves in undertones. A mere scratch on their beloved cutter was enough, it seemed, to rouse a fierce indignation; a quite irrational indignation, Mr Fitton reflected, since this was war and *Santa Brigida* was an enemy. Perhaps because she had never been in action, *Snipe*'s crew had come to accept that maintaining their ship in her state of near-perfection was their chief concern.

He marked the fall of the xebec's fifth and last shot. The invisible moon sent sufficient radiance filtering through the clouds to show him the brief white column nearly half a mile astern. That would have been fired at the forechaser's full elevation so they were far beyond its range; the grazing shot wouldn't have reached the cutter if it hadn't been for the ricochet. So that hazard was past. What would Saville do now?

To win her escape the cutter had hauled as close as she could to the wind, which was from the sou'-west, and her course was taking her towards the southern point of Majorca, now some twenty miles ahead by Mr Fitton's rough estimate. In Saville's place he would hold that course for another hour, say, to get beyond any chance of observation by the xebec, and then double back northward with the Majorcan coast below the horizon to port. And then—

He caught himself up short. He had no idea what Saville would decide to do. Once round that south point of Majorca there was a clear run to Gibraltar, perhaps five days' sailing. Would Saville consider it now impossible to fulfil his mission, and sail straight for Gib? It was of course unthinkable to ask him.

But at six bells of the middle watch part of the question, at least, was answered: the cutter was put about and headed north by east, with the light breeze over her port

155

quarter. By daybreak she was twenty miles to westward of Ciudadela with a lookout at her masthead, and the hands were hard at it scrubbing her deck.

Below in his cabin Mr Owen was sorting his wood-rasps and pots of paint in readiness for making-good the damage wrought by those sons of Belial.

2

'They'll be eighteen-pounders in a vessel of that size,' said Mr Adey, 'and she's a broadside o' ten guns. That's a tough nut for this barky to crack.'

Mr Knott licked the last morsel of burgoo from his spoon. 'Tough,' he conceded, 'but there's more ways of cracking a nut than taking a sledge-hammer to it.' He turned to Mr Fitton. 'D'ye reckon we're likely to come across her again, sir—that *Santa*?'

'Your guess is as good as mine, Mr Knott,' returned Mr Fitton cautiously.

He had been relieved from his watch-on-deck, the morning watch, ten minutes ago; Saville, in taking-over, had said nothing about his plans or about anything else.

Snipe was now moving slowly northward over a calm sea, her single jib and fully-reefed mainsail giving her no more than two or three knots before the intermittent puffs of a light southerly wind. It was a sultry overcast morning with no sparkle to it. The sun made a brazen glow behind the clouds and the leaden-hued circle of sea spread lifeless and empty—no sail or land had been sighted since daybreak. Nevertheless, the masthead lookout was being relieved every hour and told to keep his eyes moving through the whole 360 degrees. As nearly as Mr Fitton could guess, they were about a dozen miles north-east of Cape Formentor on Majorca island, and though it was improbable that *Santa Brigida* would find them again any other vessel they sighted must be assumed to be an enemy ship.

The cutter's flight and successful escape had not brought much pleasure to her crew, judging by the murmurings that had come to Mr Fitton's ears. Mr Knott, speculating about a possible future encounter, was giving vent to the feelings of the ship's company. Mr Adey, however, had no patience with heroics.

'And if we did come across her again,'

he was saying now, 'what could we do but run for it, same as we did last night? Those eighteen-pounders have twice the range of our pop-guns—aye, and twice the acc'racy.'

'Why then, we board her,' the boatswain said with a ferocious grin. 'I've heard as how the Dons don't have much stomach for cold steel.'

The gunner blew out his breath derisively. 'There's times, George Knott, when you talk a deal of nonsense. You know as well as I do we'd be blown to matchwood afore we could come alongside. And think, now—supposing the *Santa* can man both broadsides, that's a hundred men. Say another couple o' dozen to handle her and you've got odds o' four to one against us. I'm not saying nothing against our lads, but they'd need to be Jack-the-Giant-Killers with magic swords if they was to—'

'They have the sword of the Lord and of Gideon!' pronounced Mr Owen as he entered the cabin. 'And they'd be arrayed against the Whore of Babylon,' he added, wiping his paint-soiled fingers on a piece of rag.

'Easy, now, Meredith,' begged Mr Knott anxiously.

'I say unto you the Lord would fight for us,' the carpenter went on in his deep musical voice. 'Are not these Spaniards Romanists, myrmidons of the Scarlet Woman? *Esgob mawr!* If I had the rascal who grooved my counter within my grasp, look you now, he should not escape with his life!'

Mr Adey pounced on this at once.

'So you'd kill him, eh? And where'd he go? No harp and wings for him, by your way of it. You'd deliberately—deliberately, Mr Owen—send a man to Hell. Now I don't call myself a Christian, but to my mind—'

'But the damage, Mr Owen,' Mr Fitton cut in hastily. 'You succeeded with your repair?'

'I would be ashamed, Mr Fitton, to call it a repair,' the carpenter said solemnly. 'It is like unto a whited sepulchre, indeed, a sorry mess hidden under a lick of paint. No—she'll have to have a new strake there, and I misdoubt they'll have what I want at Gibraltar.'

'We want a new mainmast to my way of thinking,' said the boatswain; he turned to Mr Fitton. 'You was below, sir, when we went about and I chanced to have my

159

eye on the mast. Seemed to me there was extra whip in it so I went aloft. I reckon it's sprung—not sprung bad, though—two fathoms below the cap.'

'How did that happen?'

'Could have started in that heavy blow two days ago. And throwing her round like the captain did dodging the *Santa*'ll find out any weakness, take my word for it.'

'You've reported it?'

'Aye. Captain, he went aloft to see for hisself. He don't reckon there's much to it.'

Feet clattered on the ladder and Mr Hope put his head into the cabin, with the effect of having done so to treat its occupants to a resounding hiccup.

'Mr Fitton,' he said when he had recovered, 'Captain Saville's compliments and you'll please to join him in his cabin. You and me's to take over the deck, Mr Knott.'

The three of them went on deck. Saville moved to the hatch as soon as he saw them and went down the ladder-way. Mr Fitton, following him into the cabin, was gruffly bidden to sit down, after which the captain, seating himself opposite, placed his folded hands on the table and scowled at them in silence. After a moment Mr Fitton, who knew his man now, divined that once again Saville felt the need for conference but disliked having to share his responsibility.

'I was talking with Mr Knott, sir,' he said to break the awkward pause. 'He was telling me he thinks the mainmast is sprung.'

Saville nodded without looking up. 'Knott's a first-rate bos'n,' he growled, 'but I think he's mistaken. In any case I can do nothing about it.'

'And if this weather holds there'll be little strain on the mast.'

'If it dies away to a flat calm I'll have trouble reaching the rendezvous.'

'You'll put into Cala Roqua tonight, then, sir?'

Saville shot a sudden frowning glance at him. 'But of course, Mr Fitton,' he said stiffly. 'And tomorrow night if it proves necessary. My orders, as you are aware, admit of no alternative, and I do not question orders.'

'No, sir. I beg your pardon.'

'But I don't like it, Fitton,' Saville said quickly, dropping his stiffness. 'My presence in these waters is known, I've nowhere to hide but the open sea, and the rendezvous is watched. I see no chance of success.'

'You think the *Santa Brigida* was waiting for us?'

'What else? She was there or thereabouts at midnight.'

'Implying that Miguel Oliviera has been taken and made to disclose the time and place of the appointed rendezvous.'

'Implying also, Fitton, that my mission has already failed. That to bring *Snipe* in at Cala Roqua tonight means a futile sacrifice of my ship and her crew.'

Saville's harsh voice was unusually fraught with emotion. He smote his clenched fists together.

'This damned uncertainty it is that worries me,' he muttered with a touch of apology in his quick glance. 'If I knew for sure that Oliviera was beyond help I'd sail for Gibraltar now.'

Mr Fitton wondered for a moment whether Saville was hoping for his own expressed opinion that the chance of saving Oliviera had finally gone. But during his morning watch he had given some thought to the encounter with the *Santa Brigida* and had formed another opinion.

'I think you may be mistaken about the xebec,' he said slowly. 'She may not have been waiting for us.'

'She was there,' Saville said sharply. 'And at midnight.'

'It could have been coincidence. You yourself suggested that the Spaniards might have a vessel patrolling the Minorcan coast. And I don't think she expected to find us there.'

'Your reasons?' Saville snapped.

'*Santa Brigida* was not cleared for action when she closed us. Her gunports were unopened. If she'd expected to find an enemy vessel off Cala Roqua she'd have been ready to tackle her.'

The captain grunted. 'Possibly. Anything else?'

'When I hailed her in French,' Mr Fitton continued, 'her captain, or whoever answered me, was ready at first to believe this was a French ship. If he'd known there was to be a British ship there to take Oliviera off at midnight he'd not have credited that tale for a moment.'

Saville considered this in silence for several seconds, frowning and rubbing his chin.

'I find it hard to grant your coincidence,'

he said at last, 'but the rest holds water.
Mark this, though—*Santa Brigida* will
report that she found an enemy ship
anchored off Cala Roqua and chased her
unavailingly. She could be reporting that
to the naval base at Port Mahon at this
moment. They may well guess what we
were about.'

'By your leave, sir, we were anchored off
the bay north of Cala Roqua. And if, as
we assume, they have not yet discovered
Miguel Oliviera they'll hardly tumble to
our real purpose there. If they've heard of
this proposed invasion they might wonder
if we were reconnoitring the coast for an
invasion landing but they'd hardly expect
us to return tonight.'

Saville grunted again, whether in dis-
belief or approval it was impossible to say.
Then he got up from his chair, crouching
under the deckhead, and groped in one of
the cupboards on the bulkhead.

'In counsel,' he said over his shoulder,
'it is good to see dangers. In execution, not
to see them unless they be very great. I
don't know who said that but it's my case,
Fitton.' He set a bottle and two glasses on
the table. 'What you've just said may be
guesswork but I find it encouraging. I put

the chances as three to one against our success but we'll drink to it.'

'I would say evens, sir,' said Mr Fitton as Saville filled the glasses.

'Three to one. I don't ask better.' The captain raised his glass. 'To a successful outcome.'

'And a happy return,' added Mr Fitton conventionally.

The wine was a *verdelho* madeira and the glasses were large ones; Saville set his down half-empty and fixed a frowning stare on his lieutenant.

'So we go in tonight *nec temere nec timide*,' he said. 'The cutter cleared for action and ready for any eventuality. You'll take the cockboat inshore to bring Oliviera off.'

'Aye aye, sir.'

'There's a possibility we haven't considered. A trap on shore, an ambush.'

'That had occurred to me. We'll have to chance it.'

Saville fingered his chin. 'I could send the longboat, a dozen men, muskets.'

'They'd be useless, sir, by your leave. If Oliviera's at the rendezvous there'll be no ambush. If he's not and they've set a trap, which I think unlikely, the fewer men that fall into it the better. I'd suggest myself and a single oarsman,' Mr Fitton added. 'Dancer for preference, since he speaks some Spanish and it could conceivably be useful.'

'Very well,' Saville said after a moment's consideration.

He finished his wine and set down the glass with a rap.

'And if your hopeful speculations come to nothing,' he said harshly. 'If I'm caught and have to run for it again. We were lucky last time. A second time we may not be. I'll fight if I have to. And mark this, Fitton. I'll not strike—this vessel is not to be taken. You understand?'

'I understand, sir.'

'There's a long tradition and a true one,' Saville continued, 'that no man of my family ever hauled down his flag or cried for quarter. I don't doubt it's a tradition with the Fittons too.'

Mr Fitton grinned inwardly; this appeal to the principle of *noblesse oblige* he found, in the circumstances, amusing.

'I'll bear it in mind,' he said gravely.

'Very well. I shall close the land at dusk. There'll be gun-drill at four bells afternoon watch.' Saville rose to his feet. 'Inform Mr

Adey, if you please.'

'Aye aye, sir,' said Mr Fitton, and went on deck.

3

Towards sunset the sky began to clear a little, though the fitful and uncertain breeze blew still from westward. It was unnaturally warm even for the Mediterranean in September, that wind, like the hot breath of some invisible sea-monster; according to Mr Owen, it foretold unnatural weather. Since it was a following breeze and the cutter a light craft, there was scarcely any motion of the air on her deck and the men sweated mightily at their gun-drill. When the sun went down in a conflagration of lurid colour and she altered course to south-east, bringing the breeze on her quarter, the slight additional coolness brought a general sigh of relief from all on board.

During that day of waiting for darkness the only sail sighted had been a covey of small vessels on the northwestern horizon, and these had passed from sight in five minutes; fishing-craft, no doubt, making for some Majorcan port. The lookout was still at the masthead but now with his attention fixed chiefly on the horizon ahead, for Saville wished to confirm his position with a landfall of the coast north of Ciudadela before nightfall. Fifty feet below the lookout the cutter's deck was an orderly bustle of men.

Taking advantage of the last light of day, Saville was readying his ship for action as far as he could. The ports of all twelve guns were opened and secured, breechings and tackles freed, the sponge-and-rammers laid ready, the shot-nettings that held a dozen balls checked as to their contents. Twelve water-buckets, one to be placed at each gun, had been filled and now stood in a row amidships where Mr Knott was rigging a quick-release line to hold them upright until they were needed, and Mr Adey was cutting the length of slow-match for each. The gunner had spent an hour that afternoon filling the cloth bags of the powder-charges. Mr Owen, whose task in an engagement was that of surgeon, had cleared his little cabin and emplaced two sea-chests (which nearly filled the floorspace) to serve as an operating table.

'I have the rudiments of the business,

sir,' he had said in reply to a question from Mr Fitton, 'and for the rest I trust in the Lord.'

A buzz of subdued excitement ran among the hands as they worked—pleasurable excitement, to Mr Fitton's ear. Midshipman Hope was also excited, as an accession of his affliction showed when they met in the course of their supervising duties.

'D'you think—hup!—we'll—hup!—fight, sir?' Hope demanded, his voice a trifle shaky between the hiccups.

'I think there's an even chance, Mr Hope.'

Mr Fitton considered again this assessment and found it a fair one. All depended, as far as he could see, on whether Doctor Miguel Oliviera had or had not been taken and questioned by the Spaniards; in another few hours they would know the answer.

'Land-ho!' came from the masthead. 'Dead ahead, sir!'

Saville, beside the helm, peered at the compass-card in the fading light and straightened himself to shout orders. *Snipe* came round slowly towards the wind and was brought close-hauled on a course south-west. Her captain, having made his landfall of the projection of coast north of Ciudadela, was taking her out of sight of land again before heading south.

'Quarters!' Saville roared suddenly, and was echoed instantly by the squeal of the boatswain's pipe. 'Mr Fitton,' he added more quietly, 'I shall make a round.'

All colour had gone from the west and only the luminosity of the sky, a strange yellowish green, gave light enough to see by. They walked, Saville silent as ever, past the little groups motionless at their stations; some by sheets and halyards, the gun-crews by their guns, the warrant-officers and Midshipman Hope standing stiffly amidships. At the end of this brief inspection the captain made his only comments.

'Mr Adey, I'll have cutlasses issued. Mr Hope, see them stowed in the racks below the rail. Mr Fitton, dismiss the watch-below to get their suppers.'

He turned and stalked aft. Mr Fitton, having obeyed his order, made his way below to get his own supper in the gunroom. He reflected as he went that if it turned out that all they had to do was to take a man off a beach and sail away these weighty preparations would look, in retrospect, somewhat ludicrous. That it was not going to be quite as simple as that revealed itself well before they neared the rendezvous.

Saville's aim was to reach Cala Roqua as little before midnight as possible; he had a natural desire to spend no more time there than was necessary, having been caught at anchor last night. In making this slow approach, however, he was in Mr Fitton's opinion placing too much reliance on a sure and speedy location of Cala Roqua, for which they had only the night-fishermen's directions. No doubt the captain had made careful estimates of distance and speed so as to reach his destination at the appointed time. But speed depended on the wind; and they had hardly raised the black rim of the Minorcan coast when the cutter's mainsail gave a flap and a rattle and the wind died completely away.

Saville ordered all reefs shaken out and flying jib and outer jib hoisted, and rigged his square tops'l. But a dead calm had fallen, and *Snipe* lay scarcely moving on a sea that seemed asleep. The half-moon rose above the distant coast and with it came a sudden puff of wind from the north, setting the hands jumping to the sheets and Saville barking at the helmsman; but it died away again to nothing and the boom swung idly as before. A second puff came a few minutes later with the same result. Some of the hands for'ard started to whistle shrilly for a wind, and the boatswain's voice was raised with unusual emphasis.

'Any man as sticks his jack-knife in the mast, I'll have him up afore the captain!'

Time passed, futile breaths of air raised expectation only to mock it with their evanescence. It was an hour short of midnight and by Mr Fitton's estimate they had still ten sea-miles to sail. Saville, who had given no sign of the impatience he must be feeling, spoke suddenly and sharply.

'Mr Knott! I'll have the longboat readied for launching. Rouse out the fifty-fathom cable.'

'Aye aye, sir!'

The boatswain's response was followed by his own rapid orders and the seamen worked at the casting-off of lashings and rigging of tackles as though a hard ten-mile pull towing the cutter was something to look forward to. They were ready to swing the boat into the water when *Snipe* heeled gently over to port and her boom tugged at the mainsheet.

'Steerage way, sir!' cried the helmsman, juggling with the wheel.

'Hold the wind. Mr Knott! Belay that!'

This time the little breeze had sprung up from the south-west. It flickered once, twice, and then steadied. It was a fair wind for their present south-easterly course but it was the lightest of breezes and with every sail set the cutter could make no more than three or four knots. Still, she sheered steadily in towards the coast, while Mr Knott and his men restored longboat and cable to their places, and they had barely finished the work when two pinpricks of yellow light on the dark bulk of land opened to sight on the port beam. That was Ciudadela and they were approximately on their last night's course. Saville held on for a few minutes more before bringing the cutter closer to the wind, heading south parallel to the coast and some three-quarters of a mile from it. There was no necessity for the lead this time. The little breeze, a ghost of a wind, nevertheless held steady, and *Snipe* crept ghost-like across the water with no sound except the faint rustle of water at her bow.

The visibility was better than last night, with a few stars winking through the wisps of cloud overhead and the moon, more often visible than not, shedding some light on the indentations of the coast. Saville had posted Summers, a man with good night-sight, at the masthead and another lookout in the bows, with orders not to shout but to report on deck if they saw a vessel. No bells were being sounded and the hands had been told to keep their voices down. Mr Knott had a party standing-by ready to launch the cock-boat, and George Dancer had been apprised of his duties as oarsman. As the irregular black silhouette of the land slowly unfolded on their port hand there came from the shore an intermittent scent of vegetation wafted on the warm air.

'Can't be much farther,' Saville growled.

He had been standing motionless by the helmsman with his gaze fixed ahead, though Summers at the masthead would certainly sight that possible lurking enemy first.

'I shall anchor farther out this time, Mr Fitton,' he continued. 'You'll have a longer pull but I want more sea-room.'

'At least the conditions couldn't be better for a pulling-boat,' said Mr Fitton, his eyes on the passing coast. 'Barely a quarter-mile to go, sir,' he added quickly. 'I can see my mark.'

He had discerned the deep notch in the skyline he had noted last night. The cutter was farther off-shore than she had been then, and a telescope was useless in this light, but by cupping his eyes with his hands he could concentrate his vision. When the next dimly seen little headland was passed he knew where he was. The lanterns of the night-fishermen were not there tonight to confirm it, but here undoubtedly was the shallow bay with the dip in the cliffs above it—and now he saw the tall spike of rock on its reef, the *iglesia*. Slowly the reef passed abaft the beam, revealing behind it a narrow inlet at whose head was a glimmering patch of white.

'Cala Roqua, sir, just coming abeam,' he said, conscious that he was speaking with more certainty than he felt.

Saville didn't question it. His orders came instantly and *Snipe* turned into the wind. As her anchor splashed down, the lookout sprang down to the deck beside the captain.

'Rocks a'ead, two points on the port bow, sir,' said Summers. 'I could just make 'em out, a mile or a mile-and-a-'arf off. May be a bit of an island, like, but I couldn't—'

'Very well,' Saville snapped. 'Back to your post and keep your eyes skinned. Mr Fitton—'

'Ready, sir.'

'You've been right so far. Bring Oliviera aboard and I'll back you against Solomon.'

'Aye aye, sir.'

As he ran for'ard Mr Fitton grinned. It was relief at finding no waiting xebec off Cala Roqua, he decided, that had led to Saville's making the nearest thing to a joke he had yet heard from him.

Three minutes later he was in the sternsheets of the cockboat, heading for the distant glimmer of white under the low cliffs of the shore. It was long after midnight—how long he could only guess—but Oliviera would have sense enough to know that a sailing-vessel couldn't keep appointments to the minute. If the spy was watching from the beach he would have seen *Snipe* arrive and anchor;

the moon, when it cleared the clouds, made her conspicuous even at a mile's distance. With so light a wind Saville, in his anxiety to be ready to sail at a moment's notice, wouldn't take in sail at anchor, though he might furl his topsail. Mr Fitton glanced astern as the thought crossed his mind, and saw that the topsail was even now being taken in.

'Stretch out, sir?' asked Dancer, handling his oars from the midships thwart.

'No—steady. It's a long pull.'

'Comber Mere's longer, sir.'

'You've rowed a boat there?'

'Aye, sir, many's the time.'

As if to prove it, Dancer changed his stroke from the seaman's short pull to the long steady sweep of the inland waterman.

And the sea, with starlight and moonshine glinting on its black surface, was as smooth as a Cheshire mere. How easily it might have been otherwise! Two nights ago it would have been too rough to have pulled ashore here; and if their reconnaissance had been made tonight, instead of last night, there would have been no night-fishermen to direct them to Cala Roqua. In spite of the setbacks, the xebec and the sudden calm, it seemed to Mr Fitton that his Tutelary Genius had smiled on their efforts.

The dark skyline ahead was rising higher against the stars and the beach of white sand was clear to see. As they drew closer in he felt a bristle run up his spine and was aware of its cause. Once before Mr Fitton had approached an enemy shore in a small boat at night, though then it had been to land a secret agent, not to take one off, and the landing had been a trap from which he was lucky to escape with his life. He thought it unlikely that there was an ambush laid for him in Cala Roqua but it was still a possibility; the sword belted at his waist, the cutlass on the bottom-boards beside Dancer, would hardly get them out of it if there was but they were a comfort all the same.

Now they were passing the outer end of the reef on the port hand, the *iglesia* reef; a shorter reef, he saw, walled-in the cove on its southern side. The beach of white sand at its head was a pistol-shot away, slanting up into a dark glacis of rocks whose jagged crest was fringed with the umbrella-like outline of stone-pines.

''Vast pulling,' he told Dancer.

The boat glided on, losing way. There

was no sign of life on the beach. Above the ripple of water under the bow he could hear the lapping of the little waves on the sand, and a warm pine-scented breath came from the shore. The moon passed behind a cloud as the cockboat's forefoot nosed gently into the beach and the crags of the low rock-walls on either hand were instantly black and sinister. A dozen men could be hidden among those crags. Mr Fitton told himself he was getting timid with increasing age and stepped past Dancer to jump on to the beach.

The sand was soft above the water's edge. He walked a few paces up the beach, loosening his sword in its sheath as he went, and halted. Nothing stirred. Feeling somewhat ridiculous, he spoke loudly into the emptiness of the cove.

'Gibraltar!'

The response was immediate. A cloaked figure detached itself from the shadow of the rocks close on his right and was at his side in three strides. A firm grasp settled on his arm and a contralto voice spoke breathlessly.

'Bless you! You're late but there's a chance yet.'

It was a woman.

6 Luisa

1

Mr Fitton, his self-possession shaken, jerked his arm free and took a step backwards.

'Who the devil are you?' he demanded sharply.

The jerk had shaken back the cloak's hood and the moonlight revealed a profusion of dark hair and the face of a good-looking girl. She was as tall as himself and her chin tilted as he spoke.

'My name is Luisa O'Brien,' she said haughtily. 'And if you're the captain of the vessel yonder you've lost your manners.'

Mr Fitton lifted his cocked hat. 'Your pardon, madam, but I was not expecting to meet an English lady,' he said drily. 'I am Michael Fitton, master's mate. May I ask—'

'I'm not English, I'm British. I was born in Gibraltar. My father was an army surgeon—but all that can wait. We've little time enough if we're to help Doctor Oliviera.' She pointed an imperious finger at Dancer, standing by the boat. 'Is that all the men you have with you? Have you brought muskets? Where—'

'Miss O'Brien, I'll answer no questions until you tell me why you're here and what you know of Doctor Oliviera.'

She stamped her foot. 'Amn't I trying to tell you? Listen then. He's taken. The soldiers from Ciudadela came for him four hours ago and they've shut him in the Torre Picada. At daybreak—'

'Where is this Torre Picada?'

'In the village—San Rocque—above here. At daybreak they're going to take him to Mahon for questioning. You know what that means.'

'How do you know this?' Mr Fitton demanded.

'I hid and listened.' The girl struck her hands together impatiently. 'It's wasting time we are. They've posted two soldiers for sentries and there's three of us—there's a chance we'll find a way to get him out.'

A very long chance, thought Mr Fitton. He considered swiftly. There seemed no reason to doubt the girl's story, but what was the rest of it? How did she come to be involved in Oliviera's affairs? And to launch himself on the mad expedition she was proposing, without orders, leaving Saville in ignorance of the reason for his long absence ashore—

'Miss O'Brien,' he said firmly, 'I'm taking you on board the cutter. You can explain to Captain Saville—'

'Never!' she cried angrily. 'Do you think I'll desert him? Surely to goodness you realize it's urgent—we may have to wait hours before we get a chance to act! We leave this minute or by all the saints I go back on my own!'

Mr Fitton had to make a hard decision, and make it quickly. He could accept Luisa O'Brien's tale of Oliviera's imprisonment in the Torre Picada—some sort of watch-tower, presumably—but not her conviction that there was some hope of rescuing him. However, Oliviera was the sole objective of *Snipe*'s mission, the information he had gathered of prime importance; if there was the least chance of getting him out of the enemy's hands it must be taken. Pull back to the cutter, persuade Saville to send the longboat and a dozen armed seamen? He dismissed the idea at once. For one thing, it would take too long. For another, a minor invasion and a possible siege were altogether unthinkable.

'How far is the village?' he demanded, cutting short a bitter tirade from the girl.

'Twenty minutes,' she answered at once. 'That's if we go fast.'

He swung round. 'Dancer! Lie half-a-cable off and wait my call.'

'Aye aye, sir.'

'Your man's not coming?' Luisa exclaimed. 'But—'

'I can't leave the boat unattended.' It was their only hope of escape. 'Lead on, Miss O'Brien.'

She turned without a word and plodded quickly up the slope of yielding sand towards the dark cliff of boulders at its head, Mr Fitton at her heels. When they reached the lowest rocks she halted and stripped off her cloak, dropping it into a niche where there was already (he noted) a bundle of some sort. So far as he could see in the moonlight, she was wearing a close-fitting sleeved waistcoat of some dark material and a striped skirt reaching to just below the knee. The wide low-cut neck of the waistcoat gave ample evidence of

184

a Juno-esque bosom.

'It's a steep climb,' she said. 'You'd be better without your coat.'

'I'll manage.'

Naval uniform might save his life if the Spaniards took him.

'Come on with you, then.'

She slipped between two large boulders and began to scramble up a rocky path. It was steep enough to require the use of hands at one or two places, and so narrow that his sword rattled against the rocks on either hand.

'You'll go quieter than that higher up, I hope,' Luisa panted over her shoulder. 'We're not a circus.'

Mr Fitton made no reply; in any case, he had no breath for one.

It was very hot on the windless glacis, and he was soon regretting his coat. The uptilted wilderness of boulders through which the path wound a tortuous way presented weird shapes in the fitful moonlight and was patched with evergreen bushes and thorny plants. Aromatic scents hung heavy on the air, merged as they climbed higher in the pungent smell of the stunted pines that sprouted fantastically from interstices in the rocks. They mounted a steep rise and suddenly on their right hand a tall black column stood against the sky. Mr Fitton grabbed at and caught the girl's ankle.

'The tower!' he muttered urgently.

'Let me go!' she hissed. 'That's a *taula*—the San Rocque *taula*, a Phoenician monument. No more talk, now. The village is just beyond the trees.'

The *taula*, a square-cut monolith a dozen feet high with a slab balanced on its top, fell behind as she led the way up a rise crested with wind-bent pines. Tall shrubs, rosemary by the scent, made a screen here and behind them they crouched to look beyond.

A musket-shot away the few little houses of San Rocque clustered in a slanting fold of the hillside, white and silent in the pale moonlight. Mr Fitton could make out a rough track winding along the hill and between the houses, small garden-plots, outhouses and barns. But nearer at hand, on the same level as themselves, was the Torre Picada. He had seen its like before on the Sicilian coast, built against the Turkish pirates; a round tower, white-painted, with a conical top, some thirty feet high. The Torre was no more than a hundred paces from where they were crouching. It rose between them and the San Rocque houses, on a rough plateau of stony thickets, and on the side facing them there was no doorway. The small black oblong of an unglazed window showed just below the conical roof.

Luisa, close at his side, brought her lips within an inch of Mr Fitton's ear.

'The door's on the other side,' she whispered. 'They'll have a sentry there for sure.'

'Where are the rest of the soldiers?' he whispered back.

'In that long barn above the village. There's a score of them but they won't move before—'

Her voice stopped suddenly and her hand on his shoulder pressed him down. They lay flat, peering between the stems of rosemary. A man had come round the base of the tower, a soldier in white breeches and dark coat with a military cap like a grenadier's and a musket slung on his shoulder. He shambled slowly across the rough plateau until he caught his foot on some obstruction and nearly fell; the oath he emitted came loudly to their ears. He spent a moment or two rubbing his shin and then shambled back the way he had come and out of sight.

Into Mr Fitton's mind came the bare bones of a plan. On this side of the tower the patrolling sentry was hidden from his comrade at the doorway, if that was where he was. If he could be dealt with noiselessly that left the doorway guard, and cold steel might finish him before he could raise the alarm; the long barn was in any case a good distance from the tower. Mr Fitton's left hand tightened on the hilt of his sword as he weighed the hazards. There were a hundred yards of open hillside between where he lay and the foot of the Torre, and its tufted plants and scattered stones afforded no cover; he would have to get across that before the patrolling sentry appeared. The guard, he supposed, would be changed at intervals, and his foray mustn't clash with that because it would mean four men to deal with. There was the possibility, too, that there was more than one man on duty at the unseen door of the tower. But surprise would be on his side, and if luck (or his Tutelary Genius) was with him also the thing might be done.

Luisa was speaking, her voice scarcely audible.

'We could get to the Torre while he's gone.'

'No. What's inside the Torre—what rooms?'

'A big high room inside the door, where they store fodder for the beasts. Then up above a smaller one. Many's the time I've been up there and looked out through the window yonder.'

'Reached by a staircase?'

'By a ladder and a trapdoor. If I had a prisoner I'd put him in that top room and take the ladder away.'

If the Spaniards had any sense, thought Mr Fitton, that was what they had done. Miguel Oliviera was behind that small window. He laid a hand on the girl's arm.

'Listen,' he whispered urgently. 'This is what we're going to do. When the sentry appears again we wait until he's gone back out of sight. Then I run to the foot of the Torre and hide myself in the bushes until he returns and I can do his business for him—silently, I hope.'

He could feel her trembling. With Luisa O'Brien, he thought, it was more likely to be excitement than fear.

'When you see me wave my hat,' he

continued, 'you'll hold yourself ready to move. I shall pass behind the Torre and settle with the sentry at the doorway. Then I'll signal again and you'll come—'

'But I can help,' she broke in quickly. 'I can come to the Torre as if from my house in the village and draw the door-sentry's attention while you attack him from behind.'

Quite irrationally, this plan revolted Mr Fitton's conscience. While it was to his mind legitimate warfare to take an enemy by surprise, to cut him down while he was talking to a girl was mere assassination.

'I'll not have it,' he said abruptly. 'You'll obey my orders, Miss O'Brien.'

Her whispered reply sounded resentful. 'Very well, Mr Fitton. And you'll speak your orders quieter if you don't want us discovered.'

After this exchange they lay watching in silence. The patrolling sentry took his duties casually, it seemed. How long they waited for him Mr Fitton didn't know, but it was long enough for him to think of Saville, no doubt seething with wrathful anxiety at his prolonged absence—beginning, perhaps, to believe that he had been ambushed and taken;

and of Dancer, waiting all this time in the cockboat. His uncomfortable imaginings were cut short by Luisa's sudden grip on his wrist.

The half-moon sinking in the west had passed behind a layer of cloud, but there was light enough to see by and he had seen no sentry at the base of the Torre. Then his eye caught the cause of the girl's excitement. From the small window under the roof of the Torre a dark streak was hanging. It looked like lengths of cloth knotted together. A dark bulge appeared at its upper end—the figure of a man climbing down. He was halfway down his improvised rope when the sentry appeared coming round the foot of the tower.

The impulse to shout a useless warning was strong and indeed Luisa let out a stifled cry. But there was nothing they could do. They saw Oliviera reach the end of his improvised rope, five or six feet above the ground. The sentry, a score of paces away, saw him and unslung his musket with a yell. Oliviera let himself fall, crumpled to his knees, got up again. The musket flashed and banged, and he dropped and lay where he fell.

As the sentry ran to kneel beside

the fallen man a second soldier came running from behind the tower, screeching questions as he came. The other replied with a single shouted word.

'What does he say?' Mr Fitton questioned sharply.

The answer came on a sob. '"Dead"'.

2

It had happened so quickly—all within a few seconds—that Mr Fitton found it difficult to muster his thoughts. This was the end of their mission, and it had failed. At least Miguel Oliviera had guarded his secrets from the Spaniards to the end, or so it could be assumed. All that remained was to get back to the cutter. And the girl? Beside him Luisa was lying with her head buried in her arms, her shoulders heaving with noiseless sobbing. As he hesitated, uncertain how to comfort her, she raised her head and spoke in a low firm voice.

'I'm sorry. I was—very fond of him.'

He thought he understood; this went some way towards explaining the mystery of her involvement.

'You were lovers?' he said gently.

She gave a little choking laugh. 'And he nigh old enough to be my grandfather? I have no lover, sir!'

Somewhat abashed, Mr Fitton returned his attention to the scene at the tower. The shot had alerted the soldiers in the long barn, and men were already gathering round the two by Oliviera's body. A babel of voices was topped by the furious recriminations of an officer or sergeant. No one was likely to catch sight of them, but they were too close for comfort.

'We'd better move from here,' he muttered.

The girl wriggled back from the screening bushes and stood up. 'This way, then.'

She moved away and he got up and followed. To gain their observation-post they had left the little path, and now they rejoined it where it crossed a low ridge of rocks and bushes before winding down to the village. They were out of sight from the tower here though some of the houses were in view, dimly seen now that the moon was down. There was no light, no movement; if any of the San Rocque villagers had been awakened by the musket-shot, they had thought it wisest to stay in bed. Luisa had halted to stand looking down on the village.

'Yonder's my house,' she said, pointing. 'The farthest one. 'Tis one of my mother's properties—she was Minorcan—and there I've lived these three years with old Anna that was my nurse.' Her voice took on an elegiac tone. 'My little small house with the garden and the bougainvillea and the view over the blue, blue sea—'

She stopped, gulped, and murmured some words in Spanish which Mr Fitton didn't understand.

'Yes. Well,' he said awkwardly, 'I must return to my ship as fast as possible. You'd best wait until the men have gone from the tower before you go back there. Before we part, Miss O'Brien, I'd like to say—'

'Go back?' She had spun round to face him. ''Tis bidding goodbye to my house I am! I'm coming with you!'

'But—'

'You've lost your wits if you're thinking I'd go back,' she went on vehemently. 'I'm suspect now—hasn't the doctor been lodging with me these many weeks? Don't they know my father was British? Why, the soldiers would have taken me, too, but that I chanced to be in my garden and hid from them. No, Mr Fitton! You're sailing for Gibraltar, where I've friends, and you're taking me with you.'

Mr Fitton was bereft of speech for some seconds. What she asked, or rather stated, was impossible. What accommodation was there aboard *Snipe* for a woman? What would her captain say if he turned up with his report of failure and with a girl to be taken to Gibraltar instead of Oliviera?

'I'm sorry, Miss O'Brien, but it can't be done,' he said hastily. 'Captain Saville has given strict orders—'

'Of course it can be done!' The contralto voice was sharp with anger. 'Upon my conscience, Mr Fitton, you're mighty unhelpful! Here's a British lady in danger of death or worse and you refuse to rescue her. *Santa Maria!* Where's your Royal Navy gallantry? If your Captain Saville declines to give me passage I'd have him dismissed the Service if I was his admiral. But—' she laid a hand on the bosom of her waist-jacket—'he'll not refuse me. All I ask, sir,' she went on more quietly, 'is a word with this Captain Saville. Take me out to your ship, and if he won't let me on board you can put me ashore again.'

Mr Fitton, conscious that her request

was something more than reasonable, saw that he had no alternative.

'Very well, ma'am,' he said stiffly. 'But I must point out—'

'There we are then,' she broke in almost gaily. 'I knew you'd see sense. And I'll thank you not to "ma'am" me, Michael Fitton. We're fellow-travellers and I'm Luisa. Now come on with you.'

She set off at once down the path. Mr Fitton, following, felt slightly dazed. His experience of women, admittedly not extensive, had not included a Luisa O'Brien.

With no moonlight to show footing the rock-floored zigzags of the path were not easy to tread and he was glad of the white glimmer of Luisa's cotton stockings to prepare him for the awkward steps down. The distant hum of voices from the neighbourhood of the Torre Picada had ceased before they passed the strange capped monolith of the *taula*, where the path plunged down more steeply and his sword scraped and jarred on little rock-walls where he had to use his hands. He thought of what would have happened had his desperate plan to free Oliviera been put into action and failed, raising the alarm. At

196

least they were spared the nightmare flight and pursuit by this path that would have followed; death would have been as likely from a broken neck as from a musket-ball. Luisa was making light of the headlong descent, and he had some ado to keep up with her. Mr Fitton, who prided himself on his surefootedness, comforted himself with the reflection that she must be far more familiar with this path than he was. Another thought struck him, and he voiced it when she paused at the top of a short declivity.

'This isn't the only way from San Rocque to the shore?'

'No, indeed—there's a much easier way but it leads to the cove next to this. Sometimes at night it's used by the men who go night-fishing.'

'Yes. We saw them last night.'

'You were here last night!' she exclaimed incredulously. 'But—Doctor Oliviera was waiting—ah! He told me he heard shouting and gunfire. That was your ship?'

'We were attacked by a Spanish warship. We had to up-anchor and run for it.'

'You *ran*—from a Spaniard?'

'She was a xebec, with twenty big guns to our twelve little ones,' he said curtly.

The girl was silent for a moment. 'I know that xebec,' she said. 'I've seen her a time or two these last weeks. She's from Mahon, and I think she patrols the coast.'

'She's a reason for us to get on board as soon as may be,' said Mr Fitton.'

'And that's the true word, Michael Fitton.'

She turned and scrambled down the long step in the path at a speed he could scarcely match. Below them as they reached the top of the boulder-slope the white sand glimmered, with the grey sheet of the sea spreading from its edge. There was the cockboat a hundred yards out, and far beyond it the thin white column of *Snipe*'s sails. Luisa stopped beside the wall of rock and Mr Fitton ran on down the sand, hailing the boat as he ran. The reply came at once and the boat pulled in for the shore at a rate that raised a bow-wave at her forefoot. He was surprised that he could see such a detail as that until he realized that day was breaking; it was the little wind of dawn that raised the waves breaking at his feet.

'By Christ, sir, I thought you was took,' Dancer panted as the boat nosed into the sand. 'Are they arter you?'

'No. We're taking a lady aboard, Dancer. Haul her up a bit.'

Luisa was coming down the beach. She had draped herself in the cloak and was carrying a large bundle.

'This is Miss O'Brien,' Mr Fitton said to Dancer; and to the girl, 'Stern thwart, if you please.'

He relieved her of the bundle, dumped it in the bows, and helped her into the boat.

'What's your first name, Dancer?' Luisa asked as she settled herself in the stern-sheets.

'Er—George, mum.'

'Sure and you've had a long wait, George,' she said compassionately. 'But 'twas not our—'

'That'll do,' Mr Fitton said shortly. 'Heave.'

He and Dancer shoved the boat off and splashed into the water to climb on board. The seaman shipped his oars and Mr Fitton, seating himself beside the girl, took the tiller. The cockboat swung round and headed for the cutter a mile away.

Perhaps because she felt herself reprimanded, Luisa was silent. She sat erect and

199

self-possessed, the cloak's hood concealing her face, with her hands folded in her lap, as though, he thought, she hadn't just passed through a series of adventures that would have set any other woman swooning. As the boat drew out from the projecting reefs of the shore into open sea a light westerly breeze met them, but it had none of the freshness he would have expected at this early hour. The air was warm and heavy under a grey roof of sky that was strangely tinged with purple, and a flicker of lightning far to the southward drew his glance. He stiffened suddenly as he looked, at first taking the black shape on the glimmering water to port for a ship; but it was a rock or a small islet, close in to the coast and perhaps a mile away, and he remembered that Summers, the lookout, had reported it just before the cockboat left *Snipe*.

Luisa had seen his glance. 'The little island is Na Mora, the Moor's Head,' she told him. 'Doctor Oliviera visited it—there's a fallen *taula* there.'

'He was an antiquary?'

'Yes. He—'

She stopped, choking back a sob, and they pulled on in silence. The cutter

200

loomed out of the greyness ahead, her open gunports and brailed-up sails reminding Mr Fitton that his long and unexplained absence ashore must have given Saville a very bad time. There was still a lookout at the masthead, for his cry came clearly on the breeze.

'Deck, there! Boat approachin', sir, stabb'd quarter.'

They had come within a cable-length when the expected hail reached them, in Mr Hope's high tenor.

'Boat ahoy! What boat's that?'

'Fitton!' he shouted back. 'I've a passenger.'

When the cockboat sheered alongside Saville was standing alone at the rail, a huge dark figure; his features were not discernible in the half-light.

'Where the devil have you been, Fitton?' he growled. 'Is that Doctor Oliviera?'

Mr Fitton stood up in the sternsheets. 'Doctor Oliviera's dead, sir. We saw him shot by one of his guards as he was trying to escape. This is Miss Luisa O'Brien. She was—'

'*Who?*'

Luisa stood up and threw back her hood.

'I'm Miss O'Brien, Captain Saville,' she said firmly, 'and I'm asking you please to convey me to Gibraltar.'

It was doubtless mingled astonishment and anger that held Saville speechless for several seconds. When he spoke his harsh voice held a controlled fury.

'What is the meaning of this, Mr Fitton? Are you aware that this is a warship, not a damned ferry-boat? And you, madam, can take yourself back where you came from. I don't accommodate women in my ship!'

Mr Fitton spoke quickly. 'By your leave, sir, Miss O'Brien has much to tell about Oliviera and the information he gathered.' He hoped that was true. 'And their Lordships will no doubt require a full report. I submit that Miss O'Brien should tell us what she can.'

'And if you think,' Luisa added conversationally, 'that Miss O'Brien's going to stand chatting in this boat while you lean on your ship's rail, Captain Saville, you're much mistaken. By the sound of you you're a gentleman, but your present behaviour doesn't warrant the assumption.'

Saville stood silent and motionless for so long that Mr Fitton expected another explosion. But all that came was four curt sentences.

'You can come aboard. The cockboat stays alongside. Mr Hope, take the deck. Mr Fitton, in my cabin.'

He turned away. By the time Mr Fitton had helped the girl up over the rail the captain was halfway down the ladder-way to his cabin.

3

Grey daylight was spreading from the east but it was dark below decks and the oil-lamp was alight in Saville's cabin. The captain, already sitting at the table, pointed to the other chair without speaking as Luisa entered; he was plainly not going to make any further concessions to an intrusive female. It was oppressively warm in the cabin, and the girl unhurriedly slipped off her cloak and hung it over the chair-back before seating herself, while Mr Fitton, lacking a chair, sat on the end of Saville's sea-chest, which—so small was the cabin—put him close to the table and facing Luisa.

The smoky light of the oil-lamp allowed

him to see her face properly, for the first time. But for a chin rather square than rounded and a nose that tilted upward at its end, he thought, she would have been a beauty. Beneath level dark brows, eyes of darkest blue made a rapid survey of the cabin and then turned their steady gaze on the captain. Saville had taken one look at her Minorcan dress and averted his eyes as if in disgust.

'My ship's in hazard here,' he said abruptly now. 'We'll cut this short. First your report, Mr Fitton.'

Mr Fitton had made innumerable reports to senior officers, and he knew better than to add opinions and impressions to the bare facts. His account of his shore activities took barely a minute.

'I shall overlook the fact that you acted without orders,' Saville said coldly when he had finished. 'But you placed undue reliance on the word of a woman.'

'And that woman a total stranger—you forgot to add that, captain,' Luisa said.

There was no trace of mockery in her tone, but a smile twitched at her lips. Saville ignored her remark completely. His big angular face wore a judicial sternness.

'Now, Miss O'Brien,' he growled. 'You'll

please to tell me how you came to be at Cala Roqua. Are you a Minorcan?'

'My mother was a Minorcan lady, Captain Saville. My father was Doctor Shamus O'Brien, that was head of the garrison hospital at Gibraltar, where I was born. You're aware, of course, that Gibraltar's been British for seventy years, so I'm a British subject—I was there through the Great Siege, and I no more than a child of seven years. It was there—'

'I asked how you came to be at Cala Roqua,' Saville interrupted brusquely.

'And amn't I telling you as quick as maybe?' she countered with some impatience. 'It was there my father died, in '91. We had many friends there and my mother and I stayed on for two years. I was teaching in the English school. Then my mother, who had property in Minorca, wished to return to the land of her birth and we came to live in one of her small houses at Cala Roqua—that was five years ago.'

'Before Spain declared war on us,' put in Mr Fitton, who was listening with interest.

He received a glare from Saville for his pains. The captain rapped his knuckles on the table and switched the glare to Luisa.

'Your association with Oliviera,' he said sharply. 'Come to that.'

'Sure, and I'm coming to it this minute,' she told him equably. 'My mother died last year, rest her soul, and there was I in my cottage with Anna that was my old nurse. On a day last month there comes a Spanish antiquary to Cala Roqua seeking lodgings, a neat elderly gentleman in a bag-wig and dusty black knee-breeches, with no servant and very little luggage. His name, he told me when I'd agreed to take him in, was Doctor Miguel Oliviera and he was from Barcelona.'

'Whence had he come that day?' Saville demanded.

'I never learned. But I think—from what I learned afterwards—that it was from some place on the island where they'd begun to have suspicions of him.'

Saville frowned. 'He told you what he was doing here?'

'He told me he was making inquiry into the *taulas* of Minorca, captain.'

'What are *taulas*?'

'No one knows what they were for. Ancient relics, stone columns twice the height of a man with another stone on top. There's one at Cala Roqua and another, a fallen one, on Na Mora, which is an islet a mile down the coast from here. Some say the Phoenicians put them up, but Doctor Oliviera used to say they were far, far older than the Phoenicians.' The girl shook her head sadly. 'He was a dear man! And a real antiquary, spite of his spying. He even paid a boatman to take him out to Na Mora—'

'Pray keep to the point, Miss O'Brien!' Saville snapped. 'He told you, then, that he was a British agent, a spy?'

Luisa shrugged her shoulders. ''Twas you, captain, that asked me about the *taulas*. As to Doctor Oliviera's spying, he never told me the purpose of it but 'twasn't hard to guess. In Ciudadela there's been rumour of invasion, and a xebec from Mahon makes regular patrol of the coast. He soon discovered I was British and bit by bit let me know his troubles. He was all alone and in need of help, the poor fellow! He had more perspicacity than some men,' she added reflectively. 'He saw that I was a woman whose word could be relied on.'

The captain ignored this small gibe. He shot a glance at the chronometer on the bulkhead before speaking again.

'The rendezvous at Cala Roqua,' he said

impatiently. 'He told you of that?'

'He did so. That was when he knew he was in danger. Three days ago my house was searched, do you see, myself having gone into Ciudadela with Anna and Doctor Oliviera being out about his business. Always he took his papers with him when he left the house so they found nothing to fasten suspicion on him, but there were plenty of signs they'd been there. 'Twas then he told me of the coming of a ship to take him away, and the three nights of her coming. The first night he went down to Cala Roqua alone and you didn't come. Then—'

'I know the rest,' Saville cut in harshly. 'He told you nothing of what his investigations had discovered?'

'Nothing.' The girl paused, and Mr Fitton thought he saw her smile fleetingly. 'He only—'

'Then we waste time.' Saville's tone became stiff and formal. 'Miss O'Brien, it is my duty to thank you for the assistance you have rendered to one of His Majesty's agents. I regret that I am unable to give you a passage to Gibraltar. I see no reason to think that you are in any danger and I have no accommodation for a—for a lady.'

He half-rose from his chair. Luisa remained firmly seated.

'You'll please to hear me out, Captain Saville,' she said composedly. 'Yesterday evening the soldiers came and took him away. But in the morning he had spoken with me. "If I should be taken, señorita," says he—we spoke always in Spanish—"if I should be taken you must go to Cala Roqua at midnight. If a boat comes the word is 'Gibraltar'. You will give this to the British officer." And he hands me a sealed packet, a letter, I suppose—'

'What!' Saville sat down with a thump. 'A letter? It should have been given to me immediately you came on board, madam! Where is it?'

'Here.' She placed a hand on the bosom of her dress. 'And here it stays, captain, until you give me your word that you'll afford me passage to Gibraltar.'

While Saville was struggling to find words, Mr Fitton had time to reflect that the packet couldn't be very large, in a corsage so tightly and attractively filled.

'Damned nonsense!' The captain was positively spluttering. 'That has nothing to do with your duty, which is to give me that letter. It may be of the utmost importance to His Majesty's government. You claim to be British and yet you'd—'

'I'm half Minorcan too,' she interrupted with sudden fierceness. 'I'm thinking this letter concerns an invasion. Is it I that would welcome an army trapesing across this island—much as I hate the Spaniards? I've no duty to assist that. 'Tis to Gibraltar I'm going and this—' she tapped her breast—'will get me there.'

'But—'

Saville bit the word off short. He glared at the girl and then at Mr Fitton, whose blank countenance gave him no help. Luisa, watching them, chuckled suddenly.

''Twould be so easy,' she murmured as if to herself. 'Two strong men and one weak woman. One of you grips me tight while the other helps himself to the letter. Then you bundle me into your boat and set me ashore. You'd best gag me and tie my legs, for I'd be screaming and kicking—'

'That's enough!' Saville snapped.

He gulped down his wrath and seemed to be striving to recover his lost dignity.

'Very well,' he growled at last. 'The letter.'

She ignored his outstretched hand.

'You'll give me passage to Gibraltar?'

'Yes, since I must.'

'I've your word for that?'

'You have my word, madam.'

'I doubt I'm placing undue reliance on it but I'll take it,' Luisa said with an impish smile.

With some difficulty she wriggled her fingers down between her breasts and pulled out a crumpled paper. Saville took it from her hand without speaking. It was a single sheet three times folded and sealed with wax. There was no superscription. He broke the seal, straightened the paper, and held it near the lamp, scowling as he deciphered the spidery scrawl. Then, after a brief hesitation, he read the message aloud.

'"The information I have gathered should be of great value. So that the Spanish shall not find it if I am taken, I have hidden it beneath the *taula* on Na Mora."' He looked at the girl. 'Na Mora. That's the rock offshore a mile south of us?'

The mockery had gone from Luisa's blue eyes, and they were alight with interest.

'It is so,' she told him eagerly. 'A little small island it is and I've landed there.

You may bring your ship closer, captain, for there's deep water for a half-mile at least—'

'I'll not risk her among the reefs.'

Saville frowned and rubbed his chin irresolutely. Mr Fitton could appreciate his anxiety at this further delay. It was almost broad daylight and he was anchored off an enemy shore in plain view.

'The cockboat's alongside, sir,' he said, 'and I could be there and back in half an hour.'

'And I with you.' Luisa stood up. 'You'll not find the landing-place without me.'

Saville hesitated only for a moment.

'Very well,' he snapped. 'Two oarsmen, and waste no time.'

He rose abruptly to his feet and led the way on deck.

7 Catastrophe

1

Day had broken, but it was a strange daylight that met Mr Fitton's eyes when he followed Luisa up on deck. A leaden sea, scarcely ruffled by the light wind, stretched to dark horizons beneath a level roof of purple-grey cloud, and on the southern horizon the intermittent skeins of lightning still played. Close to eastward the rugged outline of the coast stood against the pallid sky, with the lumpish black shape of Na Mora in the middle distance and beyond it a low cliff that must (he thought) be the south-western corner of the island. Over all hung an ominous stillness, as if land and sea were waiting for something to break the spell of inaction.

The duty watch squatting or lounging in the bows sprang to attention as Saville strode for'ard barking orders. The girl had followed him, but Mr Fitton delayed to

213

deposit his sword in his cabin and then to spring down the ladder to Joe Dung's galley, where the cook was stirring a huge pot of burgoo.

'Biscuit, Joe, and sharp about it,' he demanded.

'Yes, *sah!*'

Joe seized a big tin and whipped off its lid. Mr Fitton filled his pockets.

'No burgoo, sah?'

'No time, Joe.'

He ran up on deck. Saville was at the rail with Luisa beside him and Blower was lowering himself into the cockboat. Dancer's voice came from the boat.

'What about this here bundle, sir?'

'Heave it over on to the deck,' the captain said impatiently.

'Aye aye—'

'Oh no you don't!' Luisa cut in. 'You'll hand that bundle up carefully, George Dancer, or you'll have your ears boxed. Hasn't it all my worldly goods in it?'

Mr Fitton, aware of Saville's barely suppressed wrath, hastily took the bundle from Dancer and set it on the deck.

'Miss O'Brien had better go in the bows, sir,' he said.

'Miss O'Brien can go—' the muttered

growl was sharply checked—'in the bows,' Saville finished between his teeth.

Luisa had swung herself over the rail and was already settling herself on the bow thwart. Mr Fitton dropped into the sternsheets and gave the order to shove off.

'This time, Mr Fitton, there'll be no delay,' Saville said sharply across the widening water between them.

'Aye aye, sir. Stretch out, men.'

The powerful thrusts of four oars sent the cockboat flying across the almost waveless surface. Beyond Blower's rhythmically bending shoulders, beyond Dancer's protruding ears and Luisa's dark head, the islet of Na Mora drew momently nearer and larger. It seemed to be a flattened mound of rocks surmounted by a huge boulder, but so far as he could see the boulder bore no resemblance to a woman's head, Moorish or otherwise; perhaps a likeness could be perceived from the seaward side. He could see tiny waves breaking on a few outlying rocks—the approach could be tricky—and there were plants and bushes, quite tall, growing round the base of the boulder.

With the two seamen between them there could be no conversation with the girl, and he gave a moment's thought to *Snipe*'s mission, likely after all to gain its end. For there seemed every probability that they would find the package left by Oliviera and be heading for Gibraltar within the hour. That brief voyage, indeed, would hardly be a comfortable one with Luisa and Saville at daggers drawn. There were other problems, too. She would have his cabin, he presumed, and he would take over that spare berth in the gunroom. But what about sanitary matters? She'd have to be warned when the hands proposed to relieve themselves over the lee side as they were accustomed to do whenever inclined. And some sort of privy—

'Mr Fitton!' Luisa was gesturing to starboard. 'Steer for the square block at the seaward end!'

His risen spirits inclined him to reply *aye aye, sir* but he restrained this levity and merely eased his tiller over. They were racing in close now and the square block was obvious. The islet was larger than he had thought it, perhaps a hundred yards in length though he couldn't gauge its width, and the big boulder rose from its bush-clad plinth at the end they were steering for, looming above as they neared the piled rocks of the shore. Luisa rose from her thwart and knelt in the bows.

'Stop rowing,' she said over her shoulder.

'"Vast pulling,' he interpreted, and the men, breathing heavily, rested on their oars.

'Left!' called the girl.

They rounded the square block and the cockboat nosed into a narrow creek running in between rocks, its impetus carrying them on, with Luisa's gestures directing the steersman, until the forefoot grated on the shingle of a little beach. Luisa stepped over on to the beach. Mr Fitton, following, heard a slap and what sounded very like a Spanish oath; next moment he too was assailed by a cloud of mosquitoes and was slapping at his face and neck.

'Stand by,' he said hastily to the oarsmen, and hurried after the girl.

She had clambered across a bank of rocks and plunged into the miniature jungle at the foot of the big boulder, a jungle of shoulder-high bushes. Myrtle and juniper and wild olive obstructed their progress and the footing was rough and unstable, but broken twigs here and there showed that someone had been this way before them. Fortunately the majority of the mosquitoes seemed to prefer the waterside to this almost invisible trail, for only a few determined blood-seekers remained to torment them.

Luisa, who hadn't spoken since that sharp objurgation, halted so suddenly that Mr Fitton almost collided with her.

'He's not married?' she demanded without turning.

It took him a moment to connect with her unspoken thoughts.

'Captain Saville?' he said. 'I believe he isn't married.'

'Then why doesn't he like women?'

Mr Fitton hesitated. This was no business of his.

'I know little about Captain Saville's affairs, Miss O'Brien,' he said somewhat stiffly. 'You'd better ask him yourself.'

She said nothing to this, but began to push through the bushes again. They had passed the screening bulk of the big rock and the landward extension of the islet lay before them, a tangle of rock and thicket. A short half-mile beyond its tip rose the low cliffs of the coast, and Mr Fitton saw that they were strangely coloured, almost as if they were hung with moss. Glancing to his right, he caught a glimpse between the bushes of the southern horizon; low on the dark rim of sea hung a long curtain of diffused green light, as lurid a sky as any he had seen. What it foretold he couldn't guess, but he frowned as he looked to where the cutter lay a mile to northward; a sudden westerly squall would test the anchor's holding-ground and she was on a lee shore. Then a cry from Luisa distracted his attention and he saw that they had reached the *taula*.

The huge grey rectangle of stone, four paces long and two across, lay unbroken on its bed of rocks, half buried in evergreen bushes. Its giant capstone had fallen some yards away and rested tilted against a boulder. At another time Mr Fitton would have puzzled over the impulse that had driven a lost and forgotten race to erect this enigmatic monument on so detached a site, and marvelled at the ingenuity and labour that had somehow conveyed it there. Now, however, was not the time for antiquarian musings, and Luisa was already kneeling beside the high side of the fallen column and groping beneath it.

'He'd have put it where the rain couldn't reach it,' she said, pausing to rid herself of a mosquito. 'It's the careful man he was, bless his soul!'

Mr Fitton had espied the raw spot from which a small rock had been recently uprooted, and looking along the *taula*'s side saw a rock leaning against its base. A lizard darted away from his hand as he pulled the rock aside and drew from the cavity behind it a flat package bound in oiled canvas.

''Twas for that Miguel Oliviera gave his life,' Luisa said solemnly as he held it out for her to see. 'They'll remember it to him in England, I hope.'

The name of an obscure agent obscurely dead was likely to be soon forgotten, in Mr Fitton's opinion, but he didn't say so. There was no label or address on the package but an attempt had been made to write some words on it; they seemed to be *Most Secret and Urgent*. Just possibly, he reflected, its contents might turn the fortune of war in Britain's favour. At all events, this was the end of *Snipe*'s mission—the end, too, of Saville's long anxiety for his ship's safety. The sooner she upped anchor the better.

The late Mr Sims's coat had a handy pocket in the skirt over the left thigh and the package went into it snugly. His hand felt the biscuits he had pocketed, and he took two out and gave one to the girl.

'I don't know when you last ate,' he began.

'Blessings on you, Michael Fitton!' she cried, taking it eagerly. 'I'm as hungry as Dooley's pig.'

The greenish pallor had spread to the sky overhead, and in that weird light she looked like a witch from the Underworld.

'It's a drink we need,' he told her, 'but we'll not get that until we're back on board. We'd better eat as we go.'

She nodded, turned, and began to lead the way back, munching as she pushed through the bushes. The scent of rosemary hung heavy on the air as they passed below the great rock, and a little farther on the voices of Blower and Dancer made themselves heard as they tried to deal with the mosquitoes. Their language was lower-deck expletive at its lowest, but Mr Fitton thought it unlikely that Luisa would be shocked. The cursing ceased, or was at least reduced to angry growling, when the seamen heard them approaching, and creek and boat were close below when the girl, glancing to her left, suddenly halted and pointed southward.

'A ship!' she exclaimed.

The rocks dropping to the end of the creek formed a low wall here, and looking across it he saw a small dark spot beyond the level expanse of glaucous sea. It was apparently on the horizon, so it was too big to be a ship, and seemed to be cone-shaped. There was no large island, no land of any kind, between where they stood and the coast of Africa a hundred miles away. And before his eyes—he rubbed them and stared again incredulously—the dark cone was growing skyward. A yarn he had once heard from an old seaman and disbelieved came to mind, of a smoking volcano seen rising out of the sea somewhere in the Pacific. Could he be watching the emergence of a new island? Certainly there was a tendril of what might be smoke wavering up from the cone's tip, but instead of spreading as smoke would have done this tendril remained slender as it writhed up and up until it merged with the purple-green roof of cloud—and the whole spectral apparition was no longer distant. It was moving quickly towards them.

'*Dios mio!*' breathed Luisa beside him;

and as she spoke he knew what it was.

'A waterspout,' he said. 'The first I've seen.'

'In San Rocque we call it a *vuola*,' she told him, her gaze fixed on the moving column of water. 'I saw two last September. The fishermen say they can pass quite close to a boat without harming it.'

The oncoming spout was already less than two miles away, and he could see that if it held its present straight course it would pass them well out to seaward. Its form could be likened, he thought, to that of a sandglass whose thin middle tube had been enormously lengthened, for where its upper end licked against the low clouds it widened into an inverted cone. It was moving faster than any ship, fifteen or twenty knots; and now the growing noise of its progress made itself heard, a sound between a hiss and a roar.

Startled oaths from the men down in the boat told that they had seen the snakelike spout wavering above them. Mr Fitton and the girl watched in marvelling silence as it sped past half a mile away, its muted roar and its suggestion of contained violence making contrast with the oppressive stillness of the morning and the calm of the surrounding sea. The big cone of updrawn water that formed its base appeared filled with furiously leaping waves, though apart from a ring of small breakers round its perimeter the surrounding sea was undisturbed.

Mr Fitton, turning to watch the water-spout's northward rush, stiffened suddenly and caught his breath. Luisa clutched his arm. Neither of them spoke. *Snipe*, a mile away at her anchorage, was dangerously near the path of the spout. In another five seconds they knew that it would strike her.

It happened very quickly. The cutter vanished, overwhelmed by that whirling basal cone. The writhing pipe in mid-air broke and disintegrated, the white turmoil of sea subsided. *Snipe* reappeared. She was over on her beam-ends but was slowly righting herself with her loosened sails flapping in confusion; and they saw that the upper third of her mast was gone.

2

'God be thanked!' Luisa said shakily.

Mr Fitton mentally echoed her gratitude;

to see the cutter afloat and on an even keel was an immense relief. The oaths and groans of the men in the boat evidenced a different sentiment—it was the damage to their beloved *Snipe* that was in the forefront of their minds. He cut short their jeremiads with a sharp order.

'Belay that and stand by!'

The girl was already clambering down the short glacis of rocks and he followed her, regardless now of mosquitoes.

'Will you push her off, Miss O'Brien?' he said as their feet crunched on the shingle.

'I will so.'

He scrambled past the oarsmen into the sternsheets where his weight lifted the forefoot from its groove in the shingle; Luisa applied her not inconsiderable strength in a powerful shove and swung herself into the bows in a flurry of wet skirts; the cockboat floated free.

'Back, bow. Pull, stroke. Give way both.'

The boat spun on its axis and headed out of the creek, piloted by the girl's hand-signals.

The morning light had grown and settled into a grey clarity beneath the clouded sky, where the unnatural hues that had preceded the waterspout were fast fading. A westerly breeze furrowed the sea, and across the ruffled water to northward was the cutter, a sorry sight with her decapitated mast and loosened canvas flapping in the wind. Mr Fitton frowned as they drew nearer under the lusty pulling of the oarsmen; there seemed to be no one working to clear the tangle of sail and rigging aloft. That was unlike Saville's usual promptitude in emergency. Then he saw that the hands were crowded aft, not moving about but standing and looking at the deck, though he couldn't see what they were looking at.

There was no hail for the approaching boat this time, but Midshipman Hope was at the rail when they came foaming alongside.

'By thunder I'm glad you're safe back!' he called shrilly. 'I—hup! '—I thought you'd been—'

'Where's the captain?' snapped Mr Fitton, swinging himself on to the deck as he spoke.

'Aft, sir.' Hope's blue coat and white breeches were drenched and dripping. 'He's hurt bad. Mr Owen says he's dead and the boatswain says he ain't. When that thing hit us—'

Mr Fitton was running aft and heard no more. He had to step across the boom, which with its cordage and canvas had fallen and was resting on the rail, and then the throng of men was hastily opening to let him pass. Saville lay sprawled on his back just aft of the wheel with the carpenter and the boatswain kneeling on either side of him and the gunner standing nearby. His face was covered with blood from an ugly wound across the top of his forehead, and he was unconscious.

Mr Owen, who held a bundle of bloody rags with which he made ineffectual dabs at the fallen man's face, looked up as Mr Fitton bent over him.

'I think he is gone, sir,' he said solemnly. 'The Lord gave and the Lord hath—'

'Stow your rubbish!' interrupted Mr Knott impatiently. 'Didn't I hear him give a bit of a groan just afore you spoke? 'Twas the boom gave him that swipe, sir,' he added, getting to his feet. 'When the mast went the topping-lift parted, d'ye see—'

'Let me pass!' Luisa was pushing her way aft. 'Who is hurt?—Ah, I see.'

She dropped to her knees beside Saville, pushing Mr Owen unceremoniously out of the way, and peered frowningly at the head wound. Then she reached a hand to lift one of the closed eyelids, wiped her fingers on her skirt, and sat back on her heels.

'He's alive?' demanded Mr Fitton.

'Sure he's alive. And the skull's not fractured that I can see. That's not the worst of it.' She addressed the carpenter sharply. 'Throw away those rags and get clean cloths. And bandages—surely to God you've bandages on board here. And you,' she added to the boatswain with equal sharpness, 'fetch a bucket of clean water—salt water, not out of your casks. Hurry!'

'Send a hand, Mr Knott, if you please,' Mr Fitton interposed.

He nodded at Mr Owen, who had risen and was waiting uncertainly. The two warrant-officers departed for'ard at a run and he turned to the girl.

'This is no work for you, Miss O'Brien,' he said. 'Mr Owen, ship's carpenter, is authorized to deal with wounds.'

Luisa had shifted her position and was running a hand over the lower part of Saville's left leg. She looked up angrily.

'Is it that numbskull? He'd not even noticed this leg was broken.'

'Broken?'

'I said so. The tibia—and a clean break, I hope.' She stood up. 'Listen. I'm a surgeon's daughter and I have some of his craft if little of his skill—more than a carpenter's, though, I'll warrant. Do you leave me to look after this while you look after your ship—sure and it needs it!'

'But—'

'I'll want the carpenter to help me and another one of your men,' she hurried on unheeding. 'George Dancer would suit.'

'Sir!' One of the hands watching from a few paces away had stepped forward. 'Be the cap'n dead, sir?'

'No, but he's badly hurt. Lyney, Goggin, Hunt—get the canvas off that boom and bring the boom 'midships. The rest of you get for'ard and wait orders.'

Mr Owen came trotting aft carrying a large wooden box and looking disgruntled; on his heels followed a seaman—Dancer —carrying a pailful of water. Mr Fitton accosted them.

'Mr Owen, and you, Dancer, will give Miss O'Brien all the help you can. Do as she tells you. She's a—a lady surgeon,' he added, hoping to placate the carpenter, though the statement was an impossibility.

'Aye aye, sir.' Mr Owen sounded unconvinced. 'There is no end to the wonders of the Lord, indeed.'

Mr Fitton went on for'ard, stepping quickly over the litter of blocks and cordage on the deck. Overhead the broken section of mast dangled from its stays and the shrouds sagged loosely; forestay and jib halyards lay fallen across the foredeck. To bring any kind of order to this chaos, to devise some sort of rig for what was now a useless hulk, seemed a hopeless task; yet it had to be done, and as quickly as possible.

Mr Adey bobbed up from the hatch leading to the magazine. His sallow beak-nosed face wore an expression of satisfaction.

'Charges dry as a bone,' he announced. 'Lucky we had time to batten down hatches before the spout hit us—and lucky the gunports was open, or we'd have been swamped. How's Cap'n Saville?'

'The captain's in good hands and I think he'll recover.' Mr Fitton remembered that he was temporarily in command. 'Your guns will be damp, Mr Adey. Take six hands and swab out every gun, rags round the sponge-and-rammer. See the touch-holes are dry.'

'Aye aye, sir,' said the gunner smartly, and hastened for'ard shouting names.

Mr Fitton followed him. The boatswain, surrounded by seamen, was detailing them into parties. He turned as Mr Fitton came up.

'How does the captain, sir?'

'His leg is broken and it'll be some time before he can give an order. I'm in command.' He had long forgotten that he was a passenger. 'Our need, as you're aware, is to get under way as soon as possible. We have got to get some sort of rig on her, and first we want shrouds to that stump.'

'Aye, sir, I've a plan for it,' Knott said. 'I'm just lining up the topmen for the job. Cast loose the broken part first, then get a grommet on the top o' the stump and two strops properly lashed across the crown. They'll take the shrouds, and the blocks, too. But the sails—' he paused to scratch his grey head—'even with the reefs tied down the mains'l will draw too high by a couple o' fathom, and it'd take all day to cut and seam it.'

'Unship the goose-neck and roll the foot

of the sail round the boom, Mr Knott. Then the inner jib—she won't carry more than that with mains'l reduced. You can take a fathom off the foot. Two men handy with palm and needle can seam it in twenty minutes.'

'By Christ!' Mr Knott fingered his chin. 'It might do it. But a proper bloody mess she'll look—'

'Never mind her looks. She'll sail. And I'll thank you to set about it right away, boatswain.'

'Aye aye, sir!'

Knott swung round and began to roar a string of orders that set the waiting hands jumping into action; when the last was given he went amidships to supervise the work on the mast. Mr Fitton lent a hand to the party disentangling the for'ard rigging, and when the inner jib was freed he found a clear space on the foredeck where it could be spread out and cut to his direction. Once the two seamsters were seated cross-legged and at work, sewing in from either end of the fifteen-foot width of canvas, he stood back and drew a long breath. Matters requiring immediate attention had occupied him since he returned on board, to the exclusion of all else. He needed to take stock of the wider situation.

Being a seaman his first thought was for the weather, and his glance went to the south whence the waterspout had come. That horizon was clear and the sky was brightening, the cloud-ceiling was breaking under the freshening westerly wind—nothing to fear there. The coast a mile away was devoid of human movement, and the sea on every hand was empty. He hadn't shared Saville's acute anxiety about the possible advent of an enemy ship, but now that he alone was responsible for *Snipe*'s safety, and the cutter incapable of escaping from such an encounter, the possibility seemed greater. Well, there was nothing he could do beyond what was already being done. For dealing with Saville's injuries he could only rely on Luisa O'Brien; she was a godsend for which he was duly grateful to his Tutelary Genius. As for the days to come, it took resolution even to think of them.

Despite the confidence he had used with Mr Knott, Mr Fitton knew that the undertaking that faced them when they upped anchor was hazardous in the extreme. However ingenious her improvised rig, *Snipe* was a crippled ship, incapable of holding a useful course in an adverse wind and snail-slow in a fair one. To set out on a 500–mile voyage in such a vessel, at a season when the Mediterranean was liable to sudden storms, was to invite disaster; but, again, there was nothing else he could do. He remembered the sealed packet in his coat pocket, to be delivered (he supposed) to Admiral Lord St Vincent at Gibraltar. The chances against its ever reaching him had lengthened considerably.

He went aft. The cutter was alive with noise and activity; the rattle of cordage, shout and reply, the boatswain's hoarse injunctions to a seaman at the top of the mast-stump. He avoided Mr Adey and his men busy at the starboard guns, dodged past a party shortening and splicing the shrouds on the port side, and paused a moment to watch the gooseneck being unshipped while half a dozen hands supported the 40–foot boom. Luisa's voice, sharply upraised, came to his ear.

'If you must hiccup, for mercy's sake do it without shaking!'

As he came to the after-deck, he saw that she was finishing the tying of a bandage round Saville's head while Mr

Hope, squatting behind the unconscious man, supported it, looking bashful. Saville's shoe and stocking had been stripped off and the exposed left shin showed purple and swollen.

'How is it with him?' he asked.

When she looked up he was shocked to see the signs of strain and fatigue on her face. It was not, he told himself, remembering the events of the last few hours, so very remarkable.

'Sure and I'm no grand physician,' she replied with a wan little smile, 'but the pulse is strong and he let out a groan a minute ago. 'Tis the leg's my worry. I called this officer to help me,' she added. 'We haven't been introduced.'

'Oh. Mr Midshipman Hope—Miss O'-Brien. Where's Mr Owen?'

She pushed back a drooping lock of hair, wearily. 'He's making me a pair of splints for this leg. I showed him what I wanted and he's taken the measurements.'

Mr Fitton stooped to look at Saville's face, from which most of the blood had been wiped. With the pallor and closed eyes its grimness was oddly softened.

'Shouldn't he be got into his berth?' he asked.

'Is it down that ladder, and he with a broken leg? You'd be killing him.'

'I confess I'd forgotten the ladder. Mr Hope, where's that bundle that came on board with us?'

'In the captain's cabin, sir.' Hope paused to stifle a hiccup. 'He told me to put it there for safety.'

'Very well.' Mr Fitton straightened himself. 'Miss O'Brien, you'll please to go down to that cabin at once. You'll find—'

'I'll not leave him!' she declared.

'I command here and you'll do as I say. You'll find a cupboard on the bulkhead and in it a bottle and glasses. Pour yourself a glass of wine—it's madeira—sit down at the table, and drink it. I'll stay here until you return.'

She hesitated, her lips compressed. Then she nodded, got up, and went below.

'By thunder she's a stunner, sir!' Hope said in a low voice. 'Where did she learn doctoring? How did you—'

'You'll learn in due course, Mr Hope,' Mr Fitton said severely. 'Give me your version of what happened on board here.'

'Well, sir—the larboard watch was below at their breakfast. The captain was the first to see it coming for us and he yelled—I mean he ordered—the masthead lookout down and all hands to close the hatches and then to grip something and hold on for their lives. There was no time to get the anchor up. I—hup!—I grabbed the rail and then over she went and the water smashed down.'

'You didn't see the captain knocked over?'

'Didn't see anything until she was on an even keel again. But in my opinion, sir,' Hope added sagely, 'the boom swinging across like it did knocked him against the wheel. That's how he got the broken leg.'

'You're probably right. Any damage below decks?'

'Some things went to smash-oh in the galley, sir, but Joe Dung's sorted it out—and his fire's still going.' Mr Hope, perhaps unconsciously, licked his lips. 'By thunder, I could do with a plate of burgoo if he's—'

'Sir!'

The boatswain had come aft, dodging loops of cordage and dangling rope's-ends.

'The strops is rigged satisfactory, sir,' he said, 'but there's a problem with the forestay and I'd be glad o' your opinion.'

A sudden shaft of pale sunlight pierced the clouds above the coast, falling on Luisa's head and shoulders as she came up from the cabin. Mr Fitton hesitated, but only for a second.

'I'll come now, Mr Knott,' he said.

He would have given all his considerable backpay for a draught of that madeira, but the ship came first.

3

The two double clangs from *Snipe*'s bell sounded by Mr Fitton's order but at Mr Knott's suggestion.

'It'll be a sort o' symbol, sir,' the boatswain had said. 'Give us all the feeling we're shipshape and ready for service again.'

Mr Fitton, acquiescing, thought that the sounding of the bell was a fitting mark of the final emergence of order from disorder, the needed expression of a triumph. Unremitting labour and the skill of trained men had defeated the malevolence of Nature.

It was four bells of the forenoon watch. For two hours all hands had worked as a team, coordinated and directed by the three warrant officers and Mr Fitton himself, and the cutter was as seaworthy as they could make her. Her new rigging was set up and taut, her decks were clear. The reduced jib and mainsail had been hoisted and lowered, with some necessary adjustments, and more adjustments might be required when it was seen how they drew when she was under way; but she was ready to sail and only awaited the completion of the extra lashings at the head of the shrouds which Mr Knott deemed advisable. He was supervising that task now while Mr Fitton watched the operation with a critical eye.

Mr Adey came along the deck. His thin grey hair was blown into a crest by the breeze and he looked, with his beak of a nose, like a cockatoo.

'Beg to report, sir,' he said with complacent formality. 'State of preparedness as it was afore the catastrofe, as ordered.'

'Very well, Mr Adey.'

The gunner lingered, frowning. 'That there catastrofe, sir—d'ye reckon it was the equinoctials Meredith Owen was talking of?'

'According to Miss O'Brien, waterspouts aren't uncommon off Minorca at this time of year. That's all I can tell you.'

'A kind o' local phenominy, then. Thankee, sir.'

When he had gone Mr Fitton allowed himself to lean against the rail for a moment. He felt very tired. He had been to and fro between the various working-parties, advising here, lending a hand there, his eighteen years of sea experience giving him additional authority. Only once in that busy period had he found time to visit the after-deck. Saville was still unconscious, but Luisa and Hope had contrived to place him more comfortably, fetching palliasse and blanket from his cabin and moving him farther aft so that his head was below the taffrail. Movement had been made possible by the application of Mr Owen's splints, lashed firmly to the damaged leg with strips of cloth; with care he could be slid along the deck, but not—said the girl decidedly—carried down to his cabin. Mr Owen, she added with approval, had said he would construct a shelter of wood and canvas, its roof resting on the rail, to protect him from sun or rain.

Mr Fitton reflected now that his position as acting captain could terminate at any moment. If Saville regained consciousness, it was from him that the order to up anchor and make sail must come; if he did not, he himself would have to give it, launching *Snipe* on her unchancy voyage. At least, he told himself, he could be certain that Saville would want to win clear of that anchorage at the earliest possible moment.

He found himself increasingly aware of the cutter's exposed position. The clouded sky was breaking into narrow rifts, and from time to time a ray of sunshine struck through like a spear of brilliant light specifically directed at *Snipe* to call attention to her. There were no observers on shore that he could see, no fishing-boats in the offing, no sail to be discerned on the horizons north and west and south; and yet the pointing finger of the sun disturbed him each time it came. Mr Fitton was not normally impatient with things that could not be hastened but for once impatience mastered reason.

'Mr Knott!' he roared. 'Look alive with those lashings!'

'Aye aye, sir—five minutes more!'

He regretted the shout an instant afterwards. Of course Knott was as fully aware of the urgency as he was. The lapse was no doubt due to lack of food; he had made opportunity to swallow a mouthful of madeira when he went aft, but except for a fragment of biscuit he had eaten nothing for twelve hours.

'Sir!' Hope came loping from aft. 'He's coming round, sir—the captain, I mean. He spoke a word, sir—your name. He seems to—'

He stopped and followed Mr Fitton, who was already striding aft.

Luisa, sitting on the deck beside the captain, had a half-empty wineglass in her hand.

'He's taken a sip of wine,' she said as Mr Fitton came up, 'but he seems to find it hard to speak.'

He knelt beside Saville. The captain's eyes were closed and he appeared to be unconscious, but when Mr Fitton touched his hand the eyelids half opened and he spoke in a faint whisper.

'Fitton?'

'Fitton here, sir. We found Oliviera's packet on Na Mora. I have it safe—'

Another whisper interrupted him. '*Snipe*

—what's happened—to her?'

'She lost part of her mast but we've re-rigged her.'

Mr Fitton began a terse account of the re-rigging, uncertain whether Saville, whose eyes had closed again, was hearing him or even wished to hear. He was interrupted before he had finished.

'Fitton.'

'Sir?'

'Take command. I can't—my head—'

The faint voice died away.

'Aye aye, sir.'

Mr Fitton had risen to his feet when Saville spoke again, evidently making a great effort. He tried to raise his head from the deck and his voice was a distant echo of his old peremptory growl.

'Get—sail on her—now—*now!* Course north—north—Gibraltar—'

The last word died away on a sigh. Saville's head fell back, and he relapsed into unconsciousness. Luisa bent over him. Mr Fitton spoke, crisply and rapidly.

'Mr Hope, you'll remain here. Miss O'Brien and the captain are in your charge. Miss O'Brien, when we're under way and on course your needs and comfort shall be looked to.'

Without waiting for a reply he turned and hurried for'ard. The boatswain was coming to meet him.

'Extra lashings fitted, sir,' he reported somewhat stiffly. 'I reckoned 'twas best to make sure—'

'You were right, Mr Knott, and you've done excellently. Now it's all hands to up anchor and make sail, and you'll please to take the foredeck yourself—and send Cheney aft.'

The boatswain's 'aye aye, sir' was followed instantly by the squeal of his pipe, and the hands raced to their quarters at sheets and halyards. The anchor party stood ready at the little capstan. Mr Fitton went to the helm and cast off its lashing.

'I'll take her out, Cheney,' he said as the seaman came running aft. 'Stand by—Mr Knott! Hoist away!'

The clink of the pawls began, the cutter stirred and drew to her anchor.

'Up and down, sir!'

At Mr Fitton's orders the abbreviated mainsail rose slowly up the mast and the cut-down jib—the only foresail now—followed as the anchor came to the cathead. He felt her answer as he put the wheel gently over, saw the Minorcan coast slide into sight to starboard as she turned, and steadied her on her course, due north for the present. The westerly breeze was not strong enough to raise whitecaps but she gathered way until she was making perhaps four knots. Poor *Snipe!* He thought of her old liveliness, her quick response under full sail, so different from the sluggish reaction to his pressure on the wheel-spokes now. But luck had combined with judgment to give a satisfactory sail-balance; a trifle too much weather-helm wouldn't hurt. His spirits rose. There was a chance, after all.

He handed over the wheel to Cheney and stood for a moment with his eyes on the horizon ahead, counting the slender chances that had brought *Snipe* to this final stage of her mission: the fortunate location of Cala Roqua, the narrow escape from the *Santa Brigida,* the chain of events that had led to the finding of the precious information that was the object of the mission. Fortunate, too, had been his meeting with Luisa O'Brien, without whose care Saville's chances of recovery would have been considerably less. His Tutelary Genius, it seemed, had not been unmindful of their doings. If the benevolence of that

Genius continued, affording them fair weather for the Gibraltar voyage, perhaps even providing a meeting with a British frigate to which the girl and her patient could be transferred—'

'Anchor catted, sir.' The boatswain had come aft. 'The jib's drawing fairish, but the halyard—'

He checked himself abruptly. He was facing astern and his eyes widened suddenly.

'By God!' he said. 'Look yonder, sir!'

Mr Fitton spun round. Three miles to southward, just emerging from behind the cliffs of the coast, was a ship. A ship, xebec-rigged, with three masts and a lateen sail on the mizen. It was the *Santa Brigida*.

8 The Last of *Snipe*

1

The sense of this having happened before flashed through Mr Fitton's mind and was gone. Conditions were very different this time. The xebec, with courses and topsails on fore and main masts, stood out clearly in the intermittent sunshine though she was at least three miles off; the *Snipe* of two nights ago could have left her far astern long before she could come within gunshot. But the cutter was no longer the fast and weatherly vessel she had been and there was no escape for her now—it was fight or strike.

I'll not strike, Saville had said, and he had made it an order. But that had been before they had taken a passenger on board, a woman. Was it right to doom her to almost certain death? These considerations had taken only an instant of time and Hope's startled exclamation terminated them.

'By thunder, it's the—hup!—*Santa Brigida!*'

'Mr Knott,' said Mr Fitton rapidly, 'send the hands to quarters, if you please, and stand by.'

'Aye aye, sir. And hoist colours?'

'No halyards. I'll see to it.'

He turned as the boatswain ran for'ard and went to the three by the taffrail. Saville's eyes were closed but his lips were moving.

'He heard Mr Hope,' Luisa said, looking up. 'He's trying to speak.'

He bent to get his lips close to the captain's ear and spoke clearly and urgently.

'The xebec's closing us, sir, and we can't run. We have Miss O'Brien—'

He checked himself; Saville was making a great effort to speak. His voice came very faintly and yet with an effect of vehemence.

'Fight!'

Mr Fitton lifted his head and met the girl's glance. There was a defiant light in her dark-blue eyes.

'I'd as soon be drowned as captured by the Spaniards, Mr Fitton,' she said steadily. 'Leave me here to look after him.'

Then, with a little smile, ''Tis the grand view I'll have of the battle before I go.'

He could find nothing to say to this. He touched his hat in salute and turned away.

'And you'll be needing my assistant,' she reminded him.

'Go to your quarters, Mr Hope,' he said over his shoulder, and ran down to his cabin for sword and telescope.

When he came up again the carpenter was standing by the after-hatch glaring at the distant xebec, his sheeplike countenance transformed into the face of a vengeful prophet.

'Mr Owen, hammer and nails and rouse out the colours. Send a hand aloft to nail them to the mast—the stump, that is.'

'I will do that, sir, myself, by your leave,' said Mr Owen resolutely.

'Very well.—Mr Adey! All guns load!'

The squat little 12–pounders, rumbling in and out on their trucks, made an inconsiderable thunder compared with the guns of the big ships Mr Fitton had served in. He focused the glass on the xebec. She was still more than two miles off—the cutter's four knots was at least retarding the closing of the distance—and she was hoisting her topgallants and making a sorry job of it. He could see the wisp of red and yellow fluttering at her masthead, and was surprised to note that she was towing a large boat astern; perhaps her captain intended to close and board. He pictured *Snipe* as she must appear to the Spanish captain with her obviously inefficient rig—an easy prey; well, the prey wouldn't be easy if he could help it.

A puff of smoke momentarily hid *Santa Brigida*'s bows, the report following two seconds later. *Snipe* was far beyond the range of that forechaser, of course; it was a summons to heave-to and be taken. For a moment he thought of what that would mean for them—the chance of a surgeon's care for Saville, a chance of life for Luisa and for all on board. It was a swiftly passing thought. He had his orders and he would obey them.

He gauged speed and distance and decided on his course of action. *Snipe* was incapable of strategic manoeuvring and to attempt to gain the weather-gauge would be futile, but attack must be made on her fastest point of sailing. He snapped the glass shut and rapped out his orders.

'Hands to the sheets! Cheney, port helm, and handsomely.'

Snipe came slowly round towards the wind until the luff of her makeshift sail began to shiver.

'Starboard a trifle—steady.'

Now she was heading away from the land, though not at as broad an angle as Mr Fitton could have wished. He looked astern. The xebec was slow to alter course—there were unhandy seamen aboard there—and took time to bring her bows to the north-west. Now he could see the open gunports along her flank. They were sailing on almost parallel courses and he waited until he judged he could gain no further advantage. It was little enough but it would have to serve.

'Sheets! Hard a-port!'

Round she came, so sluggishly that for one instant he thought she would miss stays, to steady with the wind over her starboard quarter, heading now for a point astern of the *Santa Brigida*. Again the xebec was slow to come about, perhaps taken by surprise by this sudden change from flight to attack, but once she was round the distance between them began to close quickly. In five minutes more *Snipe* would be within range of her 18–pounders. He glanced aloft. Mr Owen was coming slowly down the shrouds, his long grey hair floating on the breeze as if in imitation of the ensign on the mast above his head. Along the deck the lit matches smoked on the rims of the water-buckets and the men stood immobile at their guns; the boatswain and Midshipman Hope were standing a little apart, the gunner by the hatch of his magazine. The faces of all were turned towards him expectantly.

Mr Fitton detested speeches, especially before-action rodomontade, but he believed in letting men know what was expected of them. He took a pace or two for'ard and halted.

'We'll be in action in a few minutes,' he said cheerfully, 'and you'll show *Santa Brigida* yonder that we know our business. She has the range of us so we shall have to stand fire until our guns can hit her. You'll wait my word for that and then you'll fire and load, fast as you can, without further orders. Gun-captains, see your guns well pointed.' That was all he wanted to say, but he knew something more was needed. 'Only do your duty, and the Dons will find they've tackled not a snipe but an eagle.'

A somewhat lame conclusion, he felt, but it raised a lusty cheer that was prolonged until he raised his hand.

'Very well—stand to your guns. Starboard broadside, Mr Adey.'

He turned aft to stand beside the helmsman and saw Luisa, at the side of the motionless Saville, raise a hand and wave to him. He waved back and faced the fast-approaching enemy.

Santa Brigida was little more than a mile away on her converging course and quickly reducing that distance—too quickly, for she would soon be head-reaching on her quarry. Her captain had evidently realized this, and was taking in his topgallants, untidily as usual. At her present angle her guns—her port broadside—would not quite bear, but if she turned a little to starboard from her course—

As the thought crossed his mind she bore to starboard. Smoke jetted and spread from her ten port guns, a ragged broadside. It was not well aimed and the white fountains rose at varying distances, the nearest a cable-length on his beam. The check had delayed her, and when she resumed her course she was almost on his starboard quarter. He was going to bring *Snipe* within half a mile before he used his guns. Was this the moment for the turn? He decided to wait a little longer, expecting her to hold on, and the decision almost put paid to his plan. Again *Santa Brigida* checked to bring her guns to bear and again her broadside spoke in flame and smoke. This time it was better aimed. A ball screeched overhead, tearing a rent in the mainsail, and simultaneously the cutter lurched and shuddered to a hit in the fore part of her hull. But the xebec had lost way—and now was his time. Eye and brain chimed together in a lightning estimate of *Santa Brigida*'s position in five minutes' time, and his orders snapped quickly.

Snipe swung her bows to starboard and headed in to the attack.

2

From the moment when he had turned from returning Luisa's wave Mr Fitton had forgotten all else except his immediate object, which was to bring his 12–pounders to close range while incurring as little damage as possible from the xebec's longer-ranged guns. Now, as *Snipe* crawled on at her walking-pace to converge on *Santa Brigida*'s course, he remembered her ship's company and the fate that would probably overtake them in the next few minutes. A glance showed him Luisa sitting composedly under the taffrail; Saville's head was resting on her lap. Along the deck the gun-crews stood, expectantly watching him, and all the faces were familiar to him now. Blower, Lyney, Dowding, the giant Woolley—his own action had brought some or all of them to the verge of death.

Mr Owen, coming aft at a run, put an end to these unprofitable thoughts.

'Sir,' panted the carpenter, 'we are badly holed on the waterline for'ard. She is making water fast, and I cannot get at it.'

'Very well, Mr Owen.' The words struck him as peculiarly inapt. 'We shall have to—'

The roar of the xebec's broadside cut him short and he staggered as the hull reeled to a double hit. The jib flapped loose on its severed halyard—and a man was down at number one gun. He glanced quickly at the xebec, snapped 'Hold your course!' at Cheney, and ran for'ard.

Hope was standing above a shapeless bundle of bloody rags. A seaman—it was Goggin—pushed furiously past to take the dead man's place.

'Who was it?' Mr Fitton demanded.

The midshipman turned a shocked face to him. His mouth drooped open and his lower lip was trembling.

'Lyney—hup!—sir,' he said shakily. 'He —the shot took him—'

'Yes. Look to your guns, Mr Hope. Think only of your guns.'

'For Christ's sake give us the word, sor!' Goggin said between his teeth, his bearded face crimson with rage.

'In one minute, Goggin.'

He ran aft again, aware that the deck beneath him had taken on an uphill slant. The two ships had closed to much less than half a mile and *Santa Brigida* had fallen astern.

'Port half a point,' he told Cheney; and then, at the full force of his powerful voice, 'All guns—*fire!*'

The crash of the cutter's six-gun broadside was heartening after the tense waiting, and when the smoke had blown clear he saw that it had been well-aimed. A lucky shot had severed the halyard of the xebec's lateen sail and it was cascading in untidy folds to the deck, and a wide gap had appeared in her rail amidships. *Snipe*'s gunners were furiously reloading, the xebec had swung so that her guns couldn't bear—

'Sir!' Cheney's voice was urgent. 'She's steerin' queer, sir—down by the 'ead, and down more every minute.'

'She is going.' The carpenter, breathless, arrived beside them. 'Holed twice below waterline. Three feet in the forehold—'

Mr Fitton ceased to hear him. Into his mind had flashed the knowledge of what he must do—their only chance. He scarcely heard the thunder of *Snipe*'s second broadside in his preoccupation with the sequence of orders he must give—and give without losing a second. A quick glance showed another gap in the xebec's rail and then his shout rose like a trumpet-call above the rumbling of the gun-trucks.

'Cease fire! Mr Knott, two grapnels and line—we shall board; All hands—cutlasses and stand by to board her!—Mr Owen,' he added more quietly, 'get Mr Adey and the cook on deck and anyone else who's below. Cheney, steer for the xebec's bows.'

He was starting to run for'ard when Luisa's voice arrested him and he turned. She spoke calmly but with urgency.

'Get me six feet of rope. I want to tie this leg to the other.'

'I'll see to it. Don't move from there until I give the word.'

He spared a moment to admire the girl's courage and foresight as he ran on. Had he doomed her and her charge to death by drowning with that last order? *Snipe* was so heavily down by the head that her bowsprit seemed almost to touch the waves. Would she sink before she reached the *Santa Brigida*?

The hands, some stripped to the waist and all of them blackened by powder-smoke, were pulling cutlasses from the racks amid a buzz of excited talk and jest.

'Still!' he snapped. 'Dancer, cut a fathom from the jib halyards and run aft with it to Miss O'Brien. Men, you'll form a line along the starboard rail and board at my order. Yell like devils as you board. These bastards have sunk our *Snipe,* and by God we'll make 'em pay for it!' At the back of his mind was astonishment that he could talk like this. 'Mr Knott, you'll lead the after party. Mr Hope, you'll lead the fore party.'

He caught a glimpse of Hope's pale face, eyes staring wide and lips tightly set, before he dashed back to the helm again, passing the carpenter who was getting a cutlass from the rack and singing, apparently to himself, as he did so.

'The sword of the Lord and of Gideon!' chanted Mr Owen.

Cheney's bearded face was anxious. ''Ard to 'old 'er on course, sir,' he said.

'Stick to it. There's not much farther to go.'

There was indeed less than a cable-length between the two ships now. He could see the faces of Spanish seamen hurrying along *Santa Brigida*'s deck, an officer in a cocked hat on her poop. They had managed to bring her round after that swing to port and in a few seconds her guns would bear. A hundred and fifty yards—a hundred—*Snipe,* waterlogged as she was, lessened the distance with painful slowness. And here it came. The xebec's side disappeared in flame and smoke.

Santa Brigida's hull being the higher of the two and the range point-blank, most of the shot passed overhead. But a ball struck *Snipe*'s stump of a mast, snapping it off at mid height. Down came the long boom and its makeshift sail—but she had way enough to carry her on for the last few yards. Her bows were swinging away, though, and he turned angrily to the helmsman. The reprimand died on his lips. There was no helmsman. Cheney, or what had been Cheney, lay sprawled on the deck, his skull crushed by the falling boom.

He sprang to the wheel and brought her round. A pistol banged close overhead and he felt the wind of the bullet past his cheek. A dark shadow rose between him and the sky—the xebec's side.

'Grapnels!' he roared. 'Boarders away!'

Snipe's bows, the water almost level with the scuppers now, ground against the side; the grapnels soared across *Santa Brigida*'s rail; and with a deafening screech as of thirty fiends let loose the cutter's men hurled themselves after the grapnels.

Mr Fitton, pausing only to draw his sword, was nevertheless a few seconds behind the rest of the crew. Before he leaped for the gap in the rail above him he saw the carpenter gain a footing on the muzzle of an 18-pounder, his grey hair blowing in the wind and his cutlass raised. An instant later the blade of an invisible adversary swept down with terrible force, striking him between neck and shoulder, and he fell back without a cry, into the narrow gap of water between the two vessels. Then Mr Fitton himself was fighting for his life. A boarding-pike gouged his left thigh but his return thrust brought the pikeman hurtling past him into the water and he had gained the deck. He had time for a quick glance—most of his men had won footing on the Spaniard's deck—and after that came a period of madness.

He was never able to say how long the fight on *Santa Brigida*'s deck lasted. All around him were men slashing, struggling, falling, shouting, screaming. He parried a downward stroke and drove his point into the man's midriff. Found himself jammed chest-to-chest with a Spanish seaman and was briefly aware of a grimacing black-moustached face before he smashed his sword-hilt into it. Detached glimpses flashed in and out of sight as he stamped and slashed: Hope grappling with a man in a red cap, Joe Dung's bald head glistening in the sun while he brandished a reddened cleaving-knife. There were no shots fired. If the Spaniards had muskets they hadn't had time to load them. Presumably they hadn't expected to be boarded with such ferocity, either.

For they were beginning to give ground. He swung his sword at a hatless man in a blue coat—the xebec's captain, he thought—and the man turned and ran before the stroke could fall, shouting as he went. Other shouts rose above the din. *'Snipe! Snipe!'* roared the cutter's men as they surged forward, forcing the huddled rank of Spaniards aft to the break of the poop, where some were already swarming over the rail.

Mr Fitton, with no adversary facing him, had time to collect himself. He remembered the big sea-boat he had seen towing aft. They were abandoning ship—this was victory! And he wanted no prisoners.

'Snipes!' he shouted. 'Let them go—let them go!'

He ran to the ship's side. *Snipe's* open gunports were only an inch or two above the surface. Luisa was standing at the taffrail with Saville motionless at her feet.

'Stand by to get him aboard!' he called

to her, and saw her raise a hand.

He turned, sheathing his sword, and was conscious of sudden dizziness. It cleared and he saw the deck with sprawled bodies lying here and there, Knott and the gunner herding the seamen away from their prey, the last half-dozen Spaniards clambering over the rail. He couldn't leave the deck himself and there were stronger men than he to use.

'Woolley! Blower!'

His voice sounded oddly weak to his ears but the two big seamen came across at a run. Blower was bleeding from a scalp wound but Woolley seemed unhurt.

'Get the captain and Miss O'Brien on board.'

'Aye aye, sir. But—' Woolley hesitated —'looks like you're hurt bad, sir.'

He pointed to Mr Fitton's left foot. He looked down. His stocking and the breeches above it were soaked with blood and a small pool of blood was spreading under his shoe.

'Never mind that—jump to it!'

He saw them leap down onto *Snipe*'s deck and his vision blurred. Mustn't swoon here, he told himself. The coaming of the main hatch was only a few feet away and he'd sit down for a while. He started unsteadily for it. Knott and Adey were coming towards him—far away, it seemed, in a tunnel seen through gathering mists. A tunnel that ended in total oblivion.

Slowly to Mr Fitton's returning consciousness came sounds: a splashing of water, a rhythmic swishing noise. There was a stinging pain in his left thigh. He perceived dimly that he was lying with his shoulders propped up and his legs covered by a blanket, and his vision cleared to show him a seaman with mop and bucket swabbing a deck that was certainly not *Snipe*'s deck. Recollection flooded back—the fight, the taking of *Santa Brigida*. He tried to shift his body, and pain wrenched an involuntary groan from him. Instantly there came a shout from close above him.

'Mr Knott! He's back!'

He recognized the voice. 'That's Dancer.'

'Aye, sir,' said Dancer, coming into view from behind him. 'Bos'n, he posted me here to give him a hail if you stirred. You ain't bad hurt, sir. I thought you'd like to know, you bein' a bit mazed, like,' he added apologetically.

'Thank you, Dancer. How long have I been lying here?'

'Best part o' half an hour, sir—here's the bos'n now.'

Strength was welling back into his limbs, and he could think clearly again. He felt the movement of the deck under him and heard the rustle of sails.

'We're under way?' he demanded sharply as Mr Knott halted in front of him.

'Right, sir,' said the boatswain, beaming at him. 'Tops'ls only and course nor'west pendin' orders. How's it with you now, sir?'

'Better every second. The captain?'

'In the cabin below the poop-deck, with the young lady looking after him. Can't hardly speak, sir, let alone give orders.'

'And *Snipe?*'

Mr Knott was silent for a moment, and when he spoke it was with measured solemnity.

'Five minutes after we got the captain and the young lady aboard, Dancer here—he was by the rail—calls out as she's going and we stood to watch her. You'll understand, sir, as I'd cast off the grapnels and she'd floated two or three fathoms off. She was well down by the head, as you'll remember, and her bows went under first, but she went down steady and quiet-like. Might ha' been a babby dropping off to sleep.'

Mr Fitton felt no inclination to smile at this somewhat unlikely analogy.

'She was a fine little ship,' he said.

'Aye—and kept her colours flying to the last,' Mr Knott said. 'Because why? Because the broken mast was buoyed up as she went down, d'ye see. The last thing we saw of her was the colours cocking up as she went under—like as if she was saying goodbye.'

He pulled a large spotted handkerchief from his pocket and blew his nose loudly, overcome by his own flight of fancy. Recovering himself, he glared at the seaman.

'You, Dancer! Relieve Summers at the mop—he's done his spell—only two mops in the whole ship!' he added. 'It's what you'd expect of Dagos, though.'

'What happened to the Spaniards?'

'Well, sir—' Mr Knott interrupted himself. 'I'd best make a sort o' report, by'r leave.'

He squatted down on his haunches

beside Mr Fitton, who lay staring up at the dimpling canvas of the maintopsail overhead.

'When did you pass out, Sir?' he asked.

'The Spaniards were getting overside, and you were holding back *Snipe*'s men.'

'Right you are, Sir—and a pretty game me and the gunner had to hold 'em back. Fighting mad, they was. We stopped 'em, though, and next minute they was helping the Dagos across the rail—and pinching their bums to make 'em yell. The helmsman had left the wheel to run for it with the rest and the *Santa* came to the wind with her canvas flapping, so I sent Summers to the helm and gave him a course to clear the coast. By then the deck was clear of Dagos except the wounded lying about.'

'What of our own dead and wounded?' Mr Fitton demanded quickly; he should have asked that question earlier, he told himself angrily. 'You're not hurt yourself?'

'Not a scratch, Sir. 'Twasn't for want o' the Dagos' trying, neither. Mr Adey, he caught a slash on his forearm but he's tied it up and seems spry enough. There's scratches and a bloody head or two among the hands—nothing serious.

But—' Mr Knott hesitated— 'Meredith Owen's gone, Sir.'

'I know. I saw him killed. I'm sorry.'

'Aye. He was a rare one, was Meredith. But he was the only man killed, sir—in the boarding, I mean. There's Lyney and Cheney went in the poor old *Snipe* and that makes three dead against the Dagos' seven. I checked that the Dagos was dead good and proper, Sir, and put 'em over the side, quick but reverent, like.'

Mr Fitton found that he could smile inwardly at that last phrase.

'And the Spanish wounded?' he asked.

'Five, Sir, and only one of 'em bleeding serious. We tied him up—' the boatswain allowed himself a sideways grin—'with your breeches, Sir.'

'My breeches!' Mr Fitton wriggled his right leg and discovered that there were no breeches under his blanket. 'What the devil—'

'They had a cockboat slung below the poop,' the boatswain hurried on, 'and two of the wounded Dagos were fit to pull, so we got 'em all into the boat and shoved 'em off for the coast. 'Twasn't more than a couple o' miles. The other boat was halfway there by then.' He chuckled.

'Chock-a-block to the gunnels she was, and if she had so much as a foot o' freeboard I'll swallow my call. They'll make it, though—there's no sea running.'

Despite the throbbing pain of his wound Mr Fitton was able to perceive the extent of his good fortune. He had lost his ship and three good men, but he had taken a prize against odds—a prize that stood a good chance of reaching Gibraltar within a week—and Knott's forethought had spared him the nuisance of five wounded prisoners. He was wounded but he felt confident of rapid recovery. He could see little from his semi-recumbent position, but he could tell that the light wind was a fair one for their future course and the blue sky overhead boded good weather.

'The gunner and two hands is going through the 'tween-decks,' Mr Knott was saying. 'Mr Hope and the cook is taking a look at galley and stores. As for that there latrine sail,' he added, 'I've got Dowding putting a long splice in the halyard and—well, I reckon that's all my report, sir.'

'How long before we can make full sail?'

''Nother twenty minutes, I'd say. You'll

want to be away from here and on course for Gib, sir?'

'The sooner the better,' Mr Fitton said. 'Mr Knott, you've done very well. But—I'd like to know how I came to lose my breeches.'

The boatswain grinned. 'Easy told, sir. When the young woman, I mean the young lady—'

'Better call her Miss O'Brien.'

'Aye aye, sir. And she's a wonder, is Miss O'Brien. I never come across a female as game as she is. Well, soon as she comes on board, Woolley and Blower carrying the captain, she spots you lying with a deal o' blood round you and yells to me to come and stand by. Then they gets the captain into the deck cabin, and she comes running back with some cloths and kneels down to have a look at you. "Off with his breeches!" she says at once. I starts to unbutton and she fair snaps my head off. "Use your knife!" she says. "Cut them off!" So I done it, sir—and a nasty hole you've got in your thigh. Quick as lightning she mops it, pads it, gets a bandage round it, me helping. "He'll do until we can get him into a berth," she says. "Send a man to be with him when he comes round." Then back she scoots to fetch a blanket and back to the cabin to look after the captain. That's where she is now, sir. By Gummy!' the boatswain interjected suddenly. 'I clean forgot this. 'Twas in a pocket on the bloody side o' your jacket so I've cleaned it up a bit.'

He handed over a canvas-wrapped package. It was Miguel Oliviera's hard-won information; the heart and core of all the hazards of the past few days. And he had clean forgotten it himself.

'You'll please to keep that safe until it can be given to Captain Saville,' he said, handing it back. 'And Mr Knott, I'll have the ship searched for a pair of breeches as soon as we've made sail.'

'Aye aye, sir.'

Mr Adey and Midshipman Hope were crossing the deck towards them. (Mr Fitton had a fleeting vision of himself sitting wrapped in his blanket like an Eastern potentate receiving his satraps.) Mr Adey had his left arm in a sling, and the midshipman's left hand was tied up in a bloodstained rag. They made their reports. According to Mr Hope the xebec was provisioned for a week, water-casks full.

'And gallons of wine, sir,' he added. 'As

much wine as water, I should think.'

'There's a lock on the wine-store?'

'It's locked, sir—the key's in my pocket. And Joe Dung, sir, is readying the mess-deck—there's bread and cheese, both fresh. No rum, though, or beer.'

'We'll make an issue of wine. Mr Adey?'

Mr Adey had found no one below decks. He had also examined deck and hull for damage and had found the only damage caused by *Snipe*'s broadside was the breakages in the rail. He turned to look at the two splintered gaps as he spoke, and so did the boatswain.

'Meredith Owen would ha' made a good repair job there, Mr Knott,' said the gunner solemnly.

'He would that, Mr Adey,' returned the boatswain with equal solemnity. 'If there's harps and wings up aloft, like he said, I reckon he's got 'em.'

A hoarse roar from aft put an unsuitable end to the carpenter's epitaph.

'That's Dowding, sir,' the boatswain said. 'They're ready to reeve that latrine halyard. The hands is all on deck, most of 'em up for'ard getting some square-rig tips from Witt and Bolsover. You'll be giving the orders, sir?'

'Yes. Sound two peeps on your call when you're ready. I'll have courses and topgallants on her to start with.'

'Aye aye, sir.'

Mr Knott trotted away aft, and Mr Fitton looked up at the other two.

'We've three masts now instead of one. Mr Adey, take charge of the mainmast, if you please. Mr Hope—foremast.'

They duly responded and turned to go to their allotted posts; but the midshipman took two paces and then stopped, his puppy-dog-like face beaming.

'Sir!' he said diffidently.

'Well?'

'Did you notice, sir? Not a single hiccup—and there hasn't been one since we boarded!'

'My felicitations, Mr Hope!' Mr Fitton called after him as he turned and ran on for'ard.

He eased his shoulders on the hatch-coaming. The dull throbbing pain of his wound was easy enough to bear, but it was galling to be here and see nothing but spars and rigging. Surely he could stand with the aid of a stick—Knott should find him one. He must rouse-out the Spanish captain's charts. The present course, taking *Santa*

Brigida away from the Minorcan coast, would do for an hour or two, but then he must lay a proper one. That would be if Saville continued unfit to take command. If he recovered sufficiently—

'And how do you find yourself now, Michael Fitton?'

Luisa O'Brien had come up unheard and was kneeling on the deck beside him.

'How does Captain Saville?' he asked at once.

She pushed back a lock of dark hair from her forehead and the gesture showed her weariness, but her answer came firm and clearly.

'Sure I am that the getting him on board here did his broken leg no good at all. Five minutes ago he came out of his swoon and spoke just one word—*"Snipe?"*—like that. I had to tell him she was sunk. He closed his eyes then and hasn't opened them since. I hope and pray he's asleep.' She shook her untidy hair and spoke more briskly. 'Now let's have a look at you.'

She reached for the bottom edge of the blanket. Mr Fitton instinctively gripped the top edge.

'Miss O'Brien,' he began; and stopped, not knowing what to say next.

Their eyes met and suddenly she burst out laughing.

'Holy Mary! Don't be a ninny, Michael —I've nursed men before this! Loose that blanket this minute!'

Reluctantly he obeyed, and she drew aside the blanket and leant over him to look at the bandaged wound. Her face was very close to his; it showed the signs of fatigue and there was a smudge of dirt on her cheek, but he thought he had never seen her look so beautiful. The low-cut bodice, too, revealed other beauties, and her nearness invited—

'There!' She sat back on her heels and laid the blanket over him again. 'There's for your modesty, Mr Master's Mate Fitton—and your wound's stopped bleeding. But I must get a clean dressing on it. There's cabins and to spare, though they're none too clean. Call two of your men and bid them bring a grating, and we'll get you into a nice comfortable berth—'

'I stay here,' he cut in firmly.

She had risen to her feet and now stood frowning down at him. 'I'm your nurse and you'll do as your nurse tells you, Mr Fitton.'

'I shall do as I wish, Miss O'Brien. I'm in command here—remember?'

The girl's frown slowly faded and became a smile. 'And it was to be Michael and Luisa between us—remember?'

Mr Fitton grinned. 'Give me a bit of a hoist up, Luisa, will you?' he said. 'I believe I'm starting a blister.'

'You'll treat it yourself, then, Michael.' She took him by the shoulders and pulled him so that he sat upright. 'But Captain Saville is no matter for jesting,' she added in a graver tone. 'I'm worried for him. He should have proper surgery.'

'Captain Saville's a lucky man.'

'What do you mean by that?'

She spoke so sharply that he was surprised. 'Why, fortunate to have found a nurse when he was in sore need of one.'

'Oh. Well, 'tis you are the lucky one,' she told him. 'Had that thrust been an inch more to the left you'd be a dead man by this. As it is, you've lost a lot of blood, Michael. I'm going to him now, but you'll be got into your berth in half an hour.'

She turned quickly and passed from his view. Mr Fitton sat reflecting for a long moment. Then he smiled to himself. He had doubtless lost a lot of blood, but he hadn't lost his heart. At least—not yet.

Two notes of a boatswain's call shrilled from aft and he took a deep breath.

'Hands to make sail! Courses and topgallants—let fall!'

Other voices echoed his shout, men ran up the shrouds and out on the yards. Canvas flapped down and was shaped by the wind into full-bellied sails. *Santa Brigida,* leaning from the wind, gave Mr Fitton a sight of the blue sea-horizon to northward and his heart lifted. Beyond that horizon lay Gibraltar.

3

The waters of Kingston Harbour shimmered in the sunshine of a Caribbean January, mirroring the white houses of the port and the blue Jamaican mountains beyond them and reflecting in perfect detail the masts and rigging of *HMS Abergavenny,* flagship of the West Indies Squadron, motionless at her moorings in mid-harbour. Mr Fitton stood on *Abergavenny*'s after-deck reading a letter.

The frigate *Iris* had come in yesterday

with the mails, and they had been distributed that morning. She had also brought the news of the taking of Minorca. In early November General Stuart had landed with an army of 3000 and advancing (it was said) as though he knew every inch of the island had captured its strongholds, Ciudadela and Mahon, without the loss of a single soldier. Minorca was now a British possession and Port Mahon with its invaluable harbour a British naval base. Mr Fitton heard the news with satisfaction but found his letter more interesting.

The address on its cover had given him the clue to its sender:

Michael Fitton Esquire
Master's Mate on board
His Majesty's Ship Abergavenny
West Indies Squadron

He knew only one person who would think to address him as 'Esquire'. The three sheets enclosed were close-written, but not crossed, in Saville's angular hand:

My dear Fitton,

I deeply regretted missing you at Gibraltar and hasten to write instead. The *Ganymede* 74, to which (you will recall) Miss O'Brien and myself were transferred when she intercepted *Santa Brigida* off Barcelona, had to complete her patrol as far as Cape Creux before returning to Gibraltar and was the slowest old tub imaginable into the bargain; though indeed her surgeon, an excellent man, did wonders for my leg. In consequence, I learned that you had sailed in *Thetis*, to join *Abergavenny* at Jamaica, the day before we dropped anchor at Gib. I was most sorry for this, since I had much to say to you and a great deal to thank you for.

The admiral visited me in the garrison hospital on my third day there and was very complimentary. It seems that Oliviera's documents will be of immense value to General Stuart, who sails from here with his army next month. I emphasized as strongly as I could the major part you yourself played in this mission, including the taking of *Santa Brigida,* but Lord St Vincent refused to agree that you deserved promotion, pointing out that you rated as a passenger in *Snipe.* [Here some words were heavily but inadequately scratched out; they looked like 'The miserable old'.] The admiral, however, consented to my suggestion that you should share in the prize money.

No doubt the time will come when the special merits of men of family will be recognized in considering promotions, but that time is evidently some way off.

I was made master and commander on the 1st of this month and given *Pasley* of 20 guns, 18–pounders. I strive daily to avoid comparing her unfavourably with my beloved *Snipe* and believe I may succeed in time.

It will ever be a regret to me, my dear Fitton, that you were unable to be present at my wedding. Miss O'Brien and I were married, at the garrison church here, on the last day of September. Mrs Saville has entreated me to send her kindest remembrances, to which I join my own. I trust we may one day meet again.

Believe me, with obligation and sincere thanks, yr. obedt. humble servant.

Jno. Saville
Master and Commander

Post Scriptum. The O'Briens, descended from King Brian Boru of Ireland, are of royal blood, Luisa tells me.

Mr Fitton smiled to himself and began to read the letter a second time. So there was to be no promotion for him; the command he coveted was as far off as ever. But those five days in *Santa Brigida* had been days of command, with no one to say 'aye aye, sir' to. He had captained her, shaped her course, brought her into Gibraltar—

'Mr Fitton!' barked the first lieutenant from the quarterdeck behind him.

'Sir?'

'In this ship, Mr Fitton, officers on deck-watch do not peruse their correspondence. Put that letter in your pocket.'

'Aye aye, sir,' said Michael Fitton.

The publishers hope that this book has given you enjoyable reading. Large Print Books are especially designed to be as easy to see and hold as possible. If you wish a complete list of our books, please ask at your local library or write directly to: Magna Large Print Books, Long Preston, North Yorkshire, BD23 4ND, England.

This Large Print Book for the Partially sighted, who cannot read normal print, is published under the auspices of

THE ULVERSCROFT FOUNDATION

THE ULVERSCROFT FOUNDATION

. . . we hope that you have enjoyed this Large Print Book. Please think for a moment about those people who have worse eyesight problems than you . . . and are unable to even read or enjoy Large Print, without great difficulty.

You can help them by sending a donation, large or small to:

**The Ulverscroft Foundation,
1, The Green, Bradgate Road,
Anstey, Leicestershire, LE7 7FU,
England.**
or request a copy of our brochure for more details.

The Foundation will use all your help to assist those people who are handicapped by various sight problems and need special attention.

Thank you very much for your help.

Other MAGNA Mystery Titles In Large Print

WILLIAM HAGGARD
The Vendettists

C. F. ROE
Death By Fire

MARJORIE ECCLES
Cast A Cold Eye

KEITH MILES
Bullet Hole

PAULINE G. WINSLOW
A Cry In The City

DEAN KOONTZ
Watchers

KEN McCLURE
Pestilence